GARDEN LIBRARY
PLANTING FIELDS ARBORETUM

D1264917

Donated by

MR & MRS CHARLES SPAHR

GARDEN LIBRARY
PLANTING FIELDS ARBORETUM

A CREATIVE STEP-BY-STEP GUIDE TO

GROWING
CLEMATIS

FH 217 11 5/31/2017

A CREATIVE STEP-BY-STEP GUIDE TO

GROWING
CLEMATIS

Author
Nicholas Hall

Flower Arrangements
Jane Newdick

Photographer
Neil Sutherland

WHITECAP
BOOKS

CLB 3315
This edition published 1994 by
Whitecap Books Ltd, 1086 West 3rd Street,
North Vancouver, B.C., Canada V7P 3JS
© 1994 CLB Publishing, Godalming, Surrey, England

Printed and bound in Singapore by Tien Wah Press
All rights reserved. No part of this publication may be
reproduced, stored in a retrieval system, or transmitted in
any form or by any means, electronic, mechanical,
photocopying, recording or otherwise, without the written
permission of the publisher and copyright holder.
ISBN 1-55110-159-9

Credits
Edited and designed: Ideas into Print
Photographs: Neil Sutherland
Photographic location: Treasures of Tenbury Ltd.
Typesetting: Ideas into Print and Ash Setting and Printing
Production Director: Gerald Hughes
Production: Ruth Arthur, Sally Connolly, Neil Randles

THE AUTHOR

Nicholas Hall is a Director of Treasures of Tenbury Ltd., a
company that encompasses the world famous gardens of
Burford House in Worcestershire, England. The gardens
also hold the National Collection of Clematis on behalf of
the National Council for the Conservation of Plants and
Gardens. Nicholas has spent all his working life in
horticulture, working for a variety of specialist nurseries
before joining Treasures in 1980.

THE FLOWER STYLIST

Jane Newdick worked for a major international magazine
company before branching out on her own to work from
her home in the countryside. She regularly contributes to a
number of magazines, as well as writing books on flower
arranging and using flowers in a variety of ways to create
unusual and beautiful decorations for the home. Her ideas
are featured on pages 94-105 of this book.

THE PHOTOGRAPHER

Neil Sutherland has more than 25 years experience in a
wide range of photographic fields, including still-life,
portraiture, reportage, natural history, cookery, landscape
and travel. His work has been published in countless books
and magazines throughout the world.

Half-title page: The beautiful flowers of 'Venosa Violacea'.
Title page: Putting the final touches to a colorful display.
Copyright page: The splendor of 'Mme. Julia Correvon'.

CONTENTS

Part One
GROWING CLEMATIS

Clematis is a widely distributed genus spread over many parts of the world, from the subtropical and tropical reaches of South America, the West Indies and West Africa to the temperate Northern Hemisphere, the Himalayas, China, Japan, New Zealand and North America. Because of this wide natural distribution, there are species and varieties suited to almost any growing conditions that we can offer in our gardens and greenhouses. Much has been written about the perils of clematis wilt and the complicated pruning these plants need, but if well grown, clematis are relatively disease-free and simple to cultivate. The sheer pleasure of seeing even the common variety 'Jackmanii' growing well cannot be equalled by any other plant with so little effort. With reasonable growing conditions, a little extra care after planting and a firm support, clematis will flourish with hardly any maintenance. The first part of this book opens with a brief look at the types of clematis available, from evergreens to herbaceous varieties, and then focuses on the practical aspects of growing them to perfection. Advice on choosing good plants and providing the right kind of soil is followed by practical demonstrations of how to prune various types of clematis, how to recognize common pests and diseases, raising clematis from seed and propagating them from cuttings and layers, and how to produce new hybrids to delight your family and friends.

Left: The double blooms of Clematis macropetala.
Right: C. orientalis *'Bill Mackenzie'* and red *'Niobe'*.

The anatomy of a clematis

It is always helpful to know something about the botanical features of a plant in order to achieve the best results when growing it in the garden. Clematis are members of the same family as the buttercups, anemones and thalictrums, and require the same rich growing conditions. If you examine any of these flowers, their resemblance to each other soon becomes apparent. They have all lost their petals in favor of colorful sepals. (On a tomato, the sepals are the green growth at the top that is discarded.) The double flowers found in clematis are in fact colorful, but deformed, stamens that have evolved to look like petals. The fruits of the clematis also bear a striking similarity to those of the buttercups. However, in the clematis the style, which sits above the seed, continues to grow and becomes a tufted seedhead, a means of seed dispersal for the clematis. The common name 'Old Man's Beard' was first applied to the seedheads of the clematis and are a decorative feature in their own right. The additional feature that distinguishes clematis from other members of the family is that they are climbers, holding onto their hosts and supports by means of their leaf stems, or petioles, which twine around any suitable object.

The clematis attaches itself by means of leaf stems, or petioles, that arise from the main stem and twine around any support.

The leaves of clematis vary in shape from the large, heart-shaped leaves of early large-flowered varieties to the delicate, fernlike foliage of species such as C. aethusifolia.

In a clematis the colorful parts of the flower are not petals, but sepals. They vary in number according to species and variety.

The female part of the flower that produces the seed lies here below the style. Once pollinated, the style produces tufted heads attached to the seed.

Right: *These flowers and foliage of the well-known clematis hybrid 'Nelly Moser' are typical of the large-flowered varieties and a useful introduction to the anatomy of clematis plants in general.*

The area of stem between leaf joints is called the internode.

New buds sprout from the leaf joints, or nodes.

Above: *Two leaves are borne on either side of the main stem. Where the leaf stems, or petioles, meet the main stem, there are buds from which new shoots bearing leaves or flowers will grow.*

In most plants, this bud would consist of green sepals enclosing the colored petals that will open to form the flower. In clematis, it is these sepals that open slowly and gradually develop their color.

Colored sepals

Style - the female part of the flower.

Stamens - the male parts of the flower. In some clematis, such as the macropetalas, these become almost like petals to form double flowers.

Diversity of clematis

Coming as they do from around the world, clematis blooms have evolved in many different ways. The variation in the flowers is amazing, from the small, starlike flowers of C. *vitalba* rambling over hedges and banks to the exotic Japanese floridas. It is not just the shapes of the flowers that are so varied, but the range of colors spans the entire spectrum. From the pure blue European alpinas to the fiery red American texensis, they have all at some time been put into the garden melting pot to produce the large range of varieties and types available today. It is no surprise that given such a range of shapes and colors and with so many uses in the garden, clematis are highly popular garden plants.

Above: The small white flowers of the wild Clematis vitalba *are not as prominent as the fluffy seedheads that are often seen in the countryside.*

Below: Clematis montana *originates from the Himalayas. This vigorous grower soon covers walls, fences or trees, and its small flowers often have a wonderful scent.*

Below: The bright red, tulip-shaped flowers of Clematis texensis *'Sir Trevor Lawrence' appear in late summer and continue into the fall. They are suitable for cutting.*

Above: The exotic Japanese Clematis florida *'Alba Plena' is not as delicate as it looks. Its double white flowers continue for most of the summer.*

Below: The European species Clematis alpina *has a number of lovely hybrids, including C.a. 'Francis Rivis', shown here. It blooms in spring, producing the largest flowers in the group.*

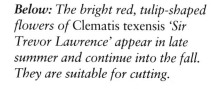

Above: The dainty yellow lanterns of Clematis tangutica *appear in late summer and are followed by tufted seedheads that are not only decorative, but attract finches and other seedeating birds to the garden.*

Above: *The early large-flowered hybrids are available in a huge range of colors, but the pure white, crimped sepals of Clematis 'Gillian Blades' take some beating.*

Given plenty of food and water, these flowers can grow as large as dinner plates.

Above: *With its huge striped flowers, Clematis 'Nelly Moser' is one of the best-loved varieties. It grows on walls and fences or in a pot, can be cut for indoors and has fluffy seedheads.*

Above: *The early-flowered Clematis macropetala is a Chinese species with double flowers. It now has a number of pink and white varieties. This group of clematis is very hardy.*

Left: *The double hybrids are probably some of the most spectacular of all garden plants. When well grown, the huge showy flowers of Clematis 'Vyvyan Pennell' look almost like those of a peony.*

15

Evergreen clematis

Some clematis varieties keep their leaves during the long winter months. In the case of the *armandii* varieties, wind is their main enemy, drying them out and causing their long, leathery leaves to become brown and brittle. For this reason, they need some protection and will do best in a sheltered corner away from icy blasts. As well as keeping their leaves, another advantage of the *armandii* varieties is their scent. They flower in early spring, releasing a wonderful vanilla fragrance to perfume the air.

The *cirrhosa* varieties, however, appear to be relatively hardy, but they do need a substantial amount of sun and winter warmth to flower. A conservatory suits them very well, but they are vigorous growers and therefore not suitable for small spaces. Although they are classified as evergreens, it is wrong to assume that they will not lose a proportion of their leaves as a result of aging. In the case of clematis, the leaves are generally lost from the bottom upwards, making the plant look rather bare. You can improve their appearance by pruning them hard back occasionally, which causes the plant to shoot from the base. Despite their need for shelter if they are to give of their best, evergreen clematis are well worth the small amount of risk involved in keeping them.

Even if they are cut back by frost, they will always come back strongly from ground level.

A selection of evergreen clematis

Clematis armandii
C.a. 'Apple Blossom'
C.a. 'Snowdrift'
Clematis cirrhosa
C.c. balearica
C.c. 'Freckles'
C.c. 'Wisley Cream'
Clematis forsteri

Right: Clematis armandii *'Snowdrift' is the best form, with larger flowers than other evergreens in the group. Its delicious vanilla scent fills the air in early spring.*

Below: Clematis cirrhosa 'Balearica' is distinguished by its fernlike leaves. If planted in a sheltered position, it is one of the earliest clematis to flower.

Below: *The flowers of* Clematis cirrhosa *'Wisley Cream' lack the red speckles seen on its relatives. On a warm winter day the flowers have a delicate scent.*

Right: Clematis armandii 'Apple Blossom' is pink in bud and opens into white, scented flowers that resemble those of apple. The young leaves are also tinged with red as they begin to grow.

Montana types

For vigor and a riot of spring color, few plants can surpass the montana group of clematis. They are capable of growing in excess of 30ft(9m), but can be kept under control by an annual shearing once flowering has finished (see page 48). Most people will be familiar with *Clematis montana* and its pink variety 'Rubens', but there is a wealth of other varieties. Many are scented, such as *Clematis montana* 'Elizabeth', and others, including *Clematis vedrariensis*, have more attractive foliage. All the montanas are useful in a variety of situations, whether it be covering old tree stumps or brightening up a dreary shed or outbuilding. Because of their vigor, they are admirably suited to growing through even quite large trees or shrubs, where their profusion of flowers will cascade downwards in a waterfall effect. Avoid applying too much rich fertilizer at the end of the growing season, as late frosts may damage new, soft growth. Montanas are not troubled by pests or disease.

Left: Clematis montana *'Tetrarose' flowers in early summer. It has the largest flowers in the group, but regrettably, no scent. The leaves have an attractive reddish tint that contrasts well with the deep pink blooms.*

Right: Clematis montana *'Elizabeth' is well suited to growing over pergolas. It can attain an eventual height of 26-33ft(8-10m). It has the added advantage that its pale pink flowers pervade the air with a delightful perfume in early spring.*

Above: Clematis chrysocoma *is available in both white and pink forms. They are less vigorous than some other montanas and also have attractive leaves.*

Right: *Prune* Clematis montana *hard back after flowering. Once this has been done, it is possible to train it to form a delicate tracery against a wall, a screen or a garden fence.*

Top montana varieties

Clematis chrysocoma
Clematis montana 'Alexander'
C.m. 'Elizabeth'
C.m. 'Freda'
C.m. 'Grandiflora'
C.m. 'Marjorie'
C.m. 'Pictons Variety'
C.m. 'Pink Perfection'
C.m. 'Tetrarose'
C.m. 'Vera'
C.m. 'Wilsonii'
Clematis vedrariensis
'Highdown'

19

Alpinas and macropetalas

This group of clematis consists of two species from opposite sides of the world and yet they are surprisingly similar. The alpinas are European and are generally single-flowered, whereas the macropetalas come from China and are doubles. Both species flower in early spring and are available in a wide range of colors, although as yet there is no yellow form. All the flowers have beautiful seedheads once flowering has finished. If you leave these on the plant they will attract a wide range of seedeating birds, and self-sown seedlings may appear around the base of the original plant.

Both the alpinas and macropetalas are some of the easiest clematis to grow and will tolerate either a sunny or a shady position without losing their flowering ability. Alpinas and macropetalas grow to an eventual height of 6-9ft(1.8-2.7m) and are very suited to growing up a low wall or through small, late-flowering shrubs, where their delicate, nodding, bell-like flowers will bring a breath of spring to your garden before more exotic varieties take their place.

Feeding the plants regularly with a high-potash fertilizer will increase the depth of color in the blooms.

Right: Clematis alpina *'Francis Rivis'* has the largest flowers in the group, each with a white central boss and deep blue sepals. The few blooms borne in summer are a bonus after the main spring flowering.

Top ten varieties

Clematis alpina *'Burford White'*
C.a. *'Columbine'*
C.a. *'Francis Rivis'*
C.a. *'Rosy Pagoda'*, C.a. *'Ruby'*
Clematis macropetala
C.m. *'Blue Bird'*
C.m. *'Maidwell Hall'*
C.m. *'Markham's Pink'*
C.m. *'White Moth'*

Left: Clematis alpina *'Ruby'*. All the clematis in this group have a profusion of flowers in spring and a few in late summer, and will provide an equally good display in either a sunny or shady part of the garden.

Both the alpinas and macropetalas bear attractive light green foliage throughout the summer.

Above: In common with other members of the group, the flowers of Clematis macropetala *will have a greater depth of color if the plant is grown in a cooler situation.*

21

Early large-flowered clematis

The blooms are borne on long stems, making this variety very useful for flower arrangement.

This group includes those clematis most often seen in gardens, such as 'Nelly Moser' and 'Barbara Jackman', but there are many other charming cultivars that are just as worthwhile. Several varieties are particularly rewarding, as they have a double flowering season, in early and again in late summer. Often, they also have attractive seedheads, which extends their period of interest into the early winter months. 'Kathleen Wheeler' is particularly eye-catching, with dinner plate-sized flowers of rich plum-purple and golden anthers. Its only disadvantage is that the flowers become frayed and tattered unless the plant is growing out of the wind. For a more exposed site, 'Horn of Plenty' would be more suitable. This very compact, free-flowering cultivar is ideal for small areas, such as under windows or growing through a low shrub. 'Dawn' is another free-flowering variety, but pearly pink, fading to soft white as the blooms age. For a creamy primrose white choose 'Moonlight'. To get the best color from this variety, plant it out of direct sunlight or grow it through a shrub. There are many varieties with strong pink and striped coloring. 'John Warren' is a well-colored variety with huge flowers of rich pink and carmine. Plant it out of the wind and you will be rewarded with a fabulous display for most of the summer. For a more subtle effect, plant 'Lincoln Star' in a shady spot, where its raspberry pink blooms are almost luminous. 'Fair Rosamond' is even more delicately shaded, with white flowers and a pink stripe. It is also the only large-flowered cultivar to have a scent.

Left: *'Dr. Ruppell' produces a profusion of these distinctive flowers, with their crimped, deep pink sepals, throughout the summer months.*

Right: *Clematis 'Lady Northcliffe' is one of the best blue varieties. Its compact habit makes it very suitable for growing in a container.*

Above: In early summer, the compact-growing 'Miss Bateman' is studded with well-shaped, pure white flowers with dark anthers. The later flowering is less prolific, but still worthwhile.

Above: Clematis 'Nelly Moser' is a tried and tested variety and still one of the best. It flourishes when planted in a shady position to prevent the very large blooms from fading.

Left: Clematis 'Niobe' is undoubtedly the finest red clematis and flowers almost continuously through the summer. It is also a very useful variety for growing in a container.

Top early large-flowered clematis

'Barbara Jackman', 'Dr. Ruppell'
'Elsa Spath', 'Fair Rosamond'
'Fireworks', 'Gillian Blades'
'Haku Ookan', 'Horn of Plenty'
'John Warren'
'Kathleen Wheeler',
'Lasurstern', 'Lincoln Star',
'Moonlight', 'Mrs. P.B. Truax'
'Nelly Moser', 'Niobe', 'Vino'

Doubles and semi-doubles

In this group of clematis you will find some of the most flamboyant flowers in the gardening world. They mainly produce their flowers on the wood of the previous year's growth, but have the added bonus of providing a secondary show of single flowers later in the year on the new shoots. For this reason, they only require a light pruning and generally do best in a sunny aspect. Shade tends to make the flowers turn a green color, but it is true to say that this feature often appeals to the flower arranger.

On varieties such as 'Vyvyan Pennell', the flowerheads are heavy and therefore prone to damage from wind and heavy rains. To enjoy the blooms at their best, plant them in a sheltered position, well away from the severest weather. However, one of the oldest varieties, *Clematis viticella* 'Purpurea Plena Elegans', is an exception to the rule. This vigorous variety flowers double on new wood and can be treated like any other viticella variety. It looks superb growing up a large golden conifer; the profusion of purple flowers against the foliage makes a wonderful, contrasting display in the last days of summer.

Above: Clematis 'Beauty of Worcester' is one of the best blue semi-doubles. The single flowers produced later in the season continue unabated well into the fall.

Left: The pure white 'Mrs. George Jackman' is an old but reliable variety with a compact habit and large flowers. If well grown, it can produce a wonderful column of color.

Right: In its single form, Clematis 'Duchess of Sutherland' provides one of the best late red clematis displays. The creamy yellow stamens contrast superbly with the colored sepals.

Top ten doubles

'Beauty of Worcester'
'Countess of Lovelace'
'Daniel Deronda'
'Duchess of Edinburgh'
'Jackmanii Alba'
'Mrs. George Jackman'
'Proteus', 'Royalty'
'Sylvia Denny', 'Vyvyan Pennell'

Right: Clematis *'Jackmanii Alba'* is a more vigorous variety, with bluish white, semi-double flowers followed by a profusion of smaller single blooms. An excellent variety for growing over an arch or pergola.

Below: Clematis *'Royalty'* is a new variety with a compact growth habit and exceptionally long flowering period, which make it ideally suited to growing in a container.

Summer hybrids

The clematis in this group flower on the current season's growth, which means that each year you must hack them to the ground. They can be successfully grown with plants that flower or have attractive stems in winter and early spring, when very little of the clematis is in evidence. Most of these clematis are best suited to growing in a free and easy style, rambling through trees and shrubs or scrambling in the border at ground level. Generally speaking, the individual flowers on the earlier types are larger than on the later ones, but the later-flowering clematis are very generous with their display and have such fine coloring and texture that flower size becomes irrelevant. Many of the late-flowering clematis can be used in conjunction with winter-flowering heathers to extend the useful flowering period of the border. A combination of the soft pink of 'Comtesse de Bouchaud', the deep red of 'Madame Edouard André' and 'Madame Baron Veillard', which is rose pink with a distinct mauve fringe, would make a breathtaking display in late summer. Another way to extend the interest in the garden is to use these clematis among old roses, whose main flowering is over, but which still have a few blooms left. The late clematis colors are very sympathetic with the tones of the rose blooms. 'Perle d'Azur' is one of the most desirable late clematis and 'Victoria', with its profusion of rounded, rosy purple blooms, is another contender, but do not disregard 'Jackmanii Superba', which is hard to equal for an easy, good-tempered, no-trouble variety.

Right: Clematis *'Perle d'Azur'* is the most perfect sky blue and extremely free-flowering. When grown along the top of an old stone or brick wall or climbing up a gray-toned conifer, it makes a sight that is hard to rival.

Below: Clematis *'Ville de Lyon'*, in common with many of these varieties, can become bare at the base. Try growing it through another shrub.

'Ville de Lyon' has been popular for almost a century, and rightly so, for it is seldom without a flower.

Left: Clematis *'Hagley Hybrid'* is an old and reliable variety with dusky pink flowers. It can be pruned lightly, which will make it flower much earlier.

Right: Clematis 'The President' is very well known, and has been grown for more than 100 years. This is not surprising, given its depth of color and long flowering period, which lasts through the summer and stops only at the onset of fall.

Top ten summer hybrids

'Comtesse de Bouchaud'
'Ernest Markham'
'Gipsy Queen'
'Hagley Hybrid'
'Jackmanii Superba'
'John Huxtable'
'Madame Baron Veillard'
'Madame Grange'
'Margaret Hunt', 'Ville de Lyon'

Left: With its soft pink flowers and vigorous growth, Clematis 'Comtesse de Bouchaud' should find a place in every garden, no matter how small.

Viticellas and hybrids

Below: 'Etoile Violette' has larger flowers than most viticellas, but is just as prolific. It is a very useful variety for growing along the ground, providing a splash of sumptuous color from late summer onwards.

For color in late summer and early fall, few plants can rival the viticella group of clematis. Flowering at a time when most other plants are closing down for the winter, these clematis can be used in a wide variety of ways to brighten up the garden. They flower on the current year's growth, so they need hard pruning in early spring if they are to be seen at their best, but this makes them ideally suited to scramble over winter heathers and through trees and shrubs. Viticellas can even be used as ground cover if they are allowed to ramble, but peg the shoots at intervals to avoid wind damage. Viticellas grow to about 9-12ft(2.7-3.7m), so they are very useful for covering arches and pergolas. Try growing them through roses that have finished blooming, or contrast them with other, later-blooming rose varieties. The hard pruning these clematis require makes the job of pruning the host plant easier. There are many varieties of viticella and they are available in a wide range of colors, so this makes them an essential addition to any garden. Their abundance of flowers adds welcome color during the difficult late summer period.

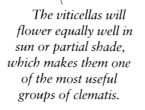

The viticellas will flower equally well in sun or partial shade, which makes them one of the most useful groups of clematis.

Top ten viticellas

Clematis viticella 'Abundance'
C. v. 'Alba Luxurians'
C. v. 'Elvan'
C. v. 'Etoile Violette'
C. v. 'Little Nell'
C. v. 'Margot Koster'
C. v. 'Minuet'
C. v. 'Purpurea Plena Elegans'
C. v. 'Royal Velours'
C. v. 'Venosa Violacea'

Left: Clematis viticella '*Mme. Julia Correvon*' is a long-flowering variety. It is easy to identify by the large gaps between the wine red sepals, which give it a rather delicate appearance.

Right: Clematis viticella '*Abundance*' associates well with foliage plants and can also scramble along the ground. Here, it is effectively teamed with Berberis *x* ottawensis.

Below: Clematis viticella '*Prince Charles*' is a new variety and one of the best late blues. Its compact growth habit makes it a useful variety for pot culture. A superb choice for the patio.

Right: Clematis viticella '*Venosa Violacea*' is very free-flowering and because its striking, purple-veined flowers are borne on long stems, it is an ideal variety for cut flower arrangements and indoor displays.

Texensis and hybrids

Until fairly recently, this group of clematis was very hard to find but today, as a result of successful modern propagation techniques, they have become more widely available and deservedly popular. The true clematis, *Clematis texensis*, originates from America as its name implies, and is a weak-growing species with small, bright scarlet, tubular flowers. Clematis breeders used this species, which in itself is not very spectacular, to cross with other varieties to produce any number of hybrids. Many of these have died out, but in recent years some fine plants have been produced. As they are not true climbers, they are best suited to scrambling over low shrubs and walls, where you can look down into their tulip-shaped flowers. They all bloom prolifically late into the summer, at a time when perhaps there is not so much color in the garden. They are generally trouble-free and not prone to clematis wilt. However, because they flower late in the season, they do appreciate a good-quality, rich soil if they are to provide enough new shoots to bear the current year's crop of flowers.

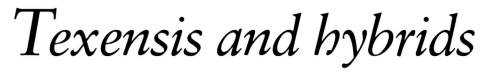

Below: 'Gravetye Beauty' is a brilliant red in color and one of the best for tulip-shaped flowers. These are held upright, making it a superb variety for growing over low shrubs so that you can look down into the flowers.

A selection of texensis hybrids

'Duchess of Albany'
'Etoile Rose'
'Gravetye Beauty'
'Ladybird Johnson'
'Pagoda'
'Sir Trevor Lawrence'
'The Princess of Wales'

Above: *The pale mauve-pink flowers of* Clematis texensis *'Pagoda' have more open sepals than other types. This gives a clue to its parentage, as it is a cross between a* Clematis texensis *variety and a viticella hybrid.*

Right: *The scrambling nature of the texensis hybrids makes them very suitable for growing through other plants. Here,* Clematis *'Princess of Wales' is growing with* Lathyrus perenne *to produce a dazzling display.*

Species clematis

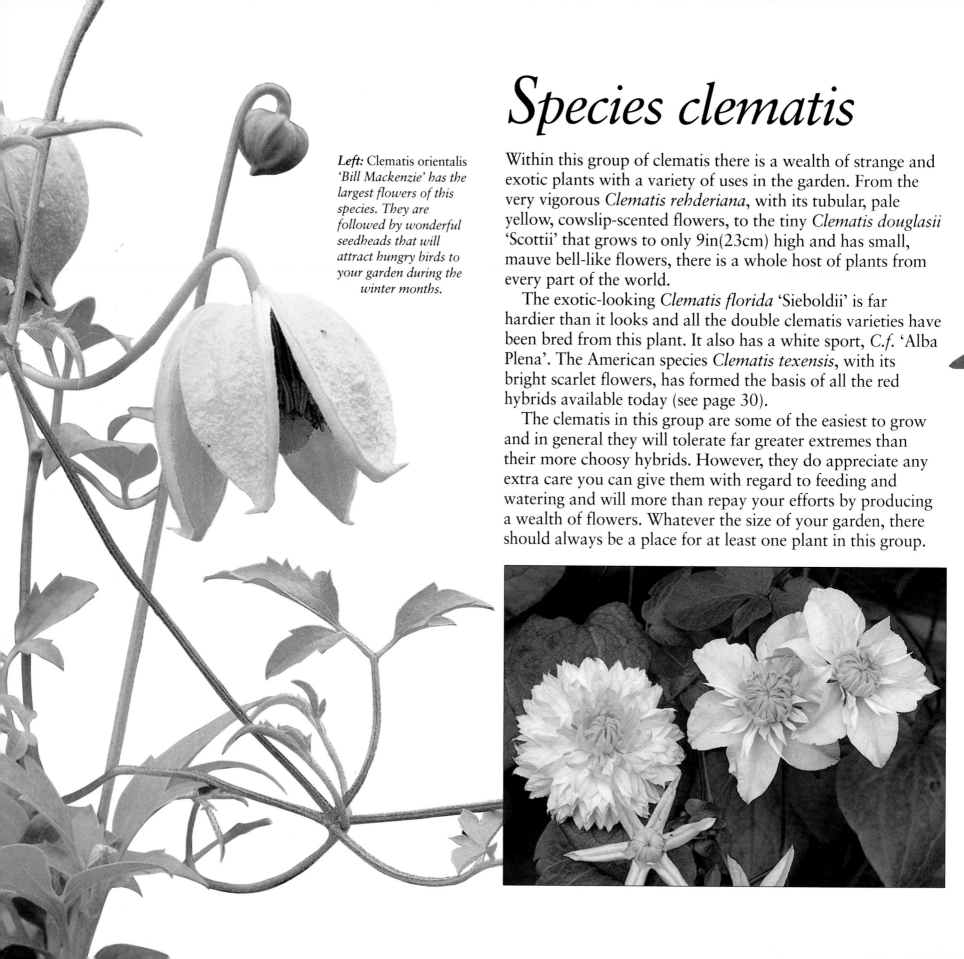

Left: Clematis orientalis 'Bill Mackenzie' has the largest flowers of this species. They are followed by wonderful seedheads that will attract hungry birds to your garden during the winter months.

Within this group of clematis there is a wealth of strange and exotic plants with a variety of uses in the garden. From the very vigorous *Clematis rehderiana*, with its tubular, pale yellow, cowslip-scented flowers, to the tiny *Clematis douglasii* 'Scottii' that grows to only 9in(23cm) high and has small, mauve bell-like flowers, there is a whole host of plants from every part of the world.

The exotic-looking *Clematis florida* 'Sieboldii' is far hardier than it looks and all the double clematis varieties have been bred from this plant. It also has a white sport, *C.f.* 'Alba Plena'. The American species *Clematis texensis*, with its bright scarlet flowers, has formed the basis of all the red hybrids available today (see page 30).

The clematis in this group are some of the easiest to grow and in general they will tolerate far greater extremes than their more choosy hybrids. However, they do appreciate any extra care you can give them with regard to feeding and watering and will more than repay your efforts by producing a wealth of flowers. Whatever the size of your garden, there should always be a place for at least one plant in this group.

Above: The beautiful pearly white blooms of Clematis 'Huldine' appear in late summer and they look particularly effective when grown through an evergreen shrub or tree, such as yew.

Left: Clematis florida 'Alba Plena' is best planted in a sunny position and allowed to grow through another climber or wall shrub to give it support and some protection from summer wind and rain.

Right: Clematis rehderiana is one of the most vigorous species and will cope with growing through quite large trees. The cowslip-scented blooms appear in late summer and hang down in large, drooping clusters.

Above: The 'passion-flowered' Clematis florida 'Sieboldii' is hardier than it appears, and if grown in a conservatory can still be in flower during the early part of the winter.

Top ten species

Clematis aethusifolia
Clematis florida 'Alba Plena'
C.f. 'Sieboldii'
Clematis 'Huldine'
Clematis jouiniana 'Praecox'
Clematis orientalis 'Bill Mackenzie'
C.o. 'L&S 13342'
Clematis rehderiana
Clematis tangutica
C.t. 'Aureolin'

Herbaceous varieties

Few gardeners have encountered herbaceous clematis, which is a pity, as there are many attractive and useful varieties. It includes those clematis that die right down for the winter before shooting again from ground level in spring. They range from big, bulky plants, such as *Clematis heracleifolia*, to *C. douglasii* 'Scottii', a dainty specimen for the front of the border. Also worth growing are *C. h. davidiana* and its clone 'Wyevale'. Their dense clusters of intensely blue flowers attract many butterflies and other beneficial garden insects. *C. jouiniana* is a cross between *C. heracleifolia* and *C. vitalba*. This variety is very sweetly scented and so smothered in blossom that the leaves are scarcely visible. It is not truly herbaceous - it dies back to about 39in(1m) in the fall - but it makes growth of up to 10ft(3m) during the season. The growth does not cling or climb, so train it to scramble on the ground or tie it in to romp over a pillar or old tree stump. Given a sunny situation in good garden soil, any of these varieties will give great pleasure during the summer.

Left: Clematis x durandii *is a semi-herbaceous variety that will scramble through shrubs or across the ground. Its leaves do not cling onto supports, so it will need fastening in if you want it to grow upwards.*

Above: Clematis integrifolia *grows to 39in(1m), sending up a cluster of shrubby stems from the crown in spring, each one ending in a nodding indigo blue flower. In an open situation it may need careful staking.*

A selection of herbaceous varieties

Clematis x durandii
Clematis x eriostemon
C. heracleifolia 'Cote d'Azur
C. h. davidiana
C. h. 'Mrs. Robert Brydon'
C. h. 'Wyevale'
Clematis recta, C. r. 'Purpurea'

Above: Clematis recta *grows to about 5ft(1.5m). Its white, scented, starlike flowers are produced in abundance during late summer and attract a wide range of butterflies, adding even more color and interest to the garden.*

Right: *Although somewhat scarce in cultivation, Clematis integrifolia 'Rosea' is well worth seeking out. C. i. 'Hendersonii' is slightly shorter than the type, but with much larger flowers that are held well above the foliage.*

Choosing a good plant

To grow clematis successfully and enjoy them at their best, it is vital to start by selecting a good specimen. A sickly plant will require endless tending and the final results are never totally satisfactory. Buy your plant from a reputable garden center or specialist grower and try to visit several suppliers to see which varieties are on offer and to assess the quality of the stock. Look for plants with unblemished, bright green foliage. Avoid any with pallid, yellowing leaves which may indicate that the plant has been in the pot too long and is lacking both nutrients and water. However, do remember that some seasonal coloration will occur as fall approaches. Examine the condition of both soil and plant support. Loose canes lead to damage at the base of the plant, its weakest point. Look at the size of the plant. Concentrate on the number of stems at the base. Clematis are such fast growers that the length of the top growth is unimportant; two or three sturdy shoots are worth extensive growth on skinny stems.

Above: *The roots of this plant are visible, which suggests that it has not been planted correctly. Always check a plant for damage at soil level, as this is an obvious route for disease.*

Above: *Strong basal shoots in early spring and a lack of top growth suggest that the plant was damaged during the winter. It will need another year before it begins flowering.*

Above: *Look for a plant with strong shoots and a good covering of potting mixture. There should be no signs of weeds or algae in the potting mixture, nor should it be hard and caked.*

GOOD PLANT
Here, the plant has reached the top of the cane, but still has leaves along the full length of the stem and has been tied in properly.

GOOD PLANT
Strong basal shoots and a well-balanced shape are more important than the height of the plant.

BAD PLANT
A plant with a single thin shoot will take longer to establish itself and may not recover if damaged.

Below: *Tempting though it may be, a clematis in flower is not necessarily the best one to buy. The energy the plant has had to invest in flowering may have been diverted away from making sufficient root growth.*

BAD PLANT
Small size is no reason to reject a plant, but here the sparseness of the leaves means that the plant is probably potbound.

Small, pale green leaves indicate a lack of feeding.

No leaves on the stem suggests that the plant has been allowed to dry out frequently.

This plant has only one main stem, which breaks higher up the plant. This shows that it was not properly pruned at potting time.

Avoid a plant in a dirty pot or one with weeds growing in the potting mixture. These are signs of neglect that could lead to problems later on.

37

Choosing the right soil

Clematis will grow in a very wide range of soil types, providing they have adequate supplies of water and nutrients. If your soil is very dry and sandy or, conversely, a heavy, cold, wet clay, you will not get the best results from your clematis unless you take some steps to improve it. If your soil is on the light side, copious applications of manure or compost will add vital humus to improve its water-retaining capabilities. However, if you garden on clay soil, then composted bark or straw manure not only help to add humus, but also opens the soil and increases the amount of air in it.

Mulching with bark or manure in early spring will also help to conserve water during the dry summer months and improve the structure of the soil. It is often said that clematis need lime in the soil, but this is largely a myth that has grown up because some wild types of clematis grow happily in chalky soils. However, the clematis that are grown today come from a wide range of countries, each with different types of soil, so generally speaking, all the varieties should thrive, given a good start.

Above: Long, fleshy clematis roots can penetrate the soil for many feet to find food and water. By improving the soil, you make it easier for the plant to form a healthy root system and thus grow more strongly.

Well-rotted cow manure is one way of adding humus. If you find it difficult to obtain, choose a proprietary form that is clean and easy to handle.

Clay soil can be very fertile, but tends to be cold and wet. Clematis do well in this type of soil, providing you improve the drainage, so that they do not become waterlogged.

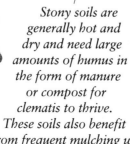

Stony soils are generally hot and dry and need large amounts of humus in the form of manure or compost for clematis to thrive. These soils also benefit from frequent mulching with organic matter, such as bark chips.

Growing clematis in containers

This mix is made from peat, grit, sand and fertilizer.

When growing clematis in pots, it is vital to use a well-balanced, proprietary potting mixture. These have been carefully researched and you should never be tempted to add anything to them that might upset the delicate balance between air and water or that could introduce weeds or disease.

Right: *Clematis will happily share the soil with a wide variety of other plants. Here, hostas and violas are planted with clematis and all will thrive in the same conditions.*

Even if you are fortunate enough to have good, loamy soil like this, you can still add well-rotted manure or compost once a year to obtain even better results from your clematis.

These bark chips last a long time before breaking down, so spread around the clematis they not only look decorative, but also reduce evaporation and prevent weeds competing for food and water.

This proprietary mixture of composted bark and manure is ideal both for sandy, well-drained soil and heavy clay soil. The manure provides humus and nutrients relatively quickly, while the bark rots down more slowly, adding substance to the soil as it does so.

39

Planting a clematis

These days, most clematis are container-grown, which means that the plant has a compact rootball that can be planted without any disturbance. There is no right or wrong time of year to plant them, but bear in mind that summer-planted clematis are in full growth while establishing and will need extra watering if they are to grow well. Having brought the plant home from the nursery or garden center, water it generously while it is still in its pot. This ensures that the rootball is completely moist before planting and also helps to prevent soil falling away when the plant is removed from the pot. While the excess water is draining away, select and prepare the site. It is vital to do this properly, as an extra five minutes spent at this stage ensures the plant's well-being in the years ahead. Once you have dug the planting hole, mix some good-quality organic material, such as old potting mixture, with the soil from the hole and add a handful of bonemeal or fish, blood and bone fertilizer. If you have access to good well-rotted manure, put some at the base of the hole and cover it with soil.

Below: *Planted correctly, a clematis will quickly establish and provide a colorful display. This is 'Lady Northcliffe'.*

3 *Fill the space around the rootball with the soil and potting mixture. Ideally, add some organic material to the soil at the base of the planting hole.*

2 *Remove the plant from its pot and carefully lower the rootball into position. Make sure that the surface of the rootball is at least 3in(7.5cm) below the soil level.*

1 *Dig a hole about twice the size of the plant and half as deep again. Be sure to break up the sides of the planting hole to allow the roots easy access into the surrounding soil.*

4 *Once the plant is in position, firm the soil down well around the base to ensure that the rootball makes close contact with the soil in the hole. Pressing down with balled fists is fine.*

Sprinkle some slug pellets around the base of the plant to ensure that it is not damaged in its early stages.

5 *As well as adding organic material to the planting hole, you can also sprinkle some around the base of the plant, keeping it away from the stem.*

Planting at the correct depth

It is important to position clematis plants at least 3in(7.5cm) deeper than the soil level in its original container. This is something you rarely do with other plants, but it is very important with clematis, as it ensures that if wilt strikes, or you run a hoe too close to the stems, the plant will regenerate from the base and grow on strongly.

This plant has been left in its pot purely to demonstrate the ideal planting depth.

6 *Give the plant another good watering to ensure that the soil is settled and there are no air pockets. Top up with more soil if necessary.*

Year round care

Once your clematis is correctly planted you have laid the foundation for its future well-being but, trouble-free though they are in general, all clematis require some attention during the year. In spring you will have to think about the annual pruning (see pages 44-49). Bear in mind that you are pruning the plant to obtain the maximum number of flowers, to contain and correct the plant's growth and to remove any non-productive, aging or damaged stems. Having pruned the clematis, check it over for damage and remove any broken or split stems. Next, tie all the shoots in to the supports using twist ties. At this stage, it is a good idea to scatter a few slug pellets at the base of the clematis or to apply a 2in(5cm) mulch of sharp sand or grit about 6in(15cm) around the plant to prevent young shoots being nibbled in the first warm days of spring. When the clematis really starts to shoot, about four to eight weeks later, check the ties again and tie in the new shoots if necessary. Add a handful of bonemeal or fish, bone and blood around the base of the plant. As the season progresses, keep training the stems along the supports; it is much easier to do this regularly than to try and sort out a bundle of full growth later on. During late spring and early summer the main problem with clematis is lack of water. The plants grow so quickly and produce such masses of large flowers that even when there have been heavy storms or you feel you have been generous with water, the average clematis will benefit from an extra bucketful every few days. Add tomato fertilizer at the recommended rate, thus supplying an extra feed when it is most needed. Apart from occasional 'running repairs' after windy weather, this is all the maintenance a clematis requires until the fall. Then, when the plant has finished flowering and before the stormy winter weather begins, reduce the weight of the top growth a little.

Leaves will naturally turn brown around the edges as they age, but this may also be a symptom of a lack of potash (potassium) in their feed. Tomato fertilizer is rich in this nutrient and is therefore ideal for clematis plants.

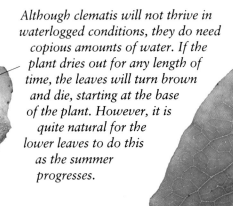

Although clematis will not thrive in waterlogged conditions, they do need copious amounts of water. If the plant dries out for any length of time, the leaves will turn brown and die, starting at the base of the plant. However, it is quite natural for the lower leaves to do this as the summer progresses.

This leaf shows clear signs that the plant bearing them is underfed and will almost certainly not flower.

Above: The thin shoots and pale green leaves are signs that this plant has been underfed and is particularly short of nitrogen. A good general fertilizer will remedy the situation.

Below: The red leaf edge is a sign of phosphate (phosphorus) deficiency. This should not be a problem on most soils provided that you topdress occasionally with manure or compost.

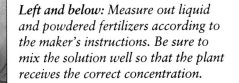

Left and below: Measure out liquid and powdered fertilizers according to the maker's instructions. Be sure to mix the solution well so that the plant receives the correct concentration.

Light pruning

This subject seems to cause gardeners endless confusion. The main rule to bear in mind when approaching these clematis is that they produce many of their flowers on the wood of the previous season's growth. This applies particularly to doubles; if pruned too hard, they will only produce single flowers, so leave as much old wood as possible to allow for maximum flowering.

The second rule is to choose the right day in early spring to carry out pruning, preferably when it is warm enough to work outside at leisure and with no distractions. If you are relaxed, you are more likely to do the job properly and with less risk of an accident, either to the plant or to yourself; secateurs are sharp and aggressive tools.

The actual pruning is very simple, if somewhat fiddly, but if you do make a mistake, remember the third golden rule, which is 'Don't panic'. The worst that can happen is that the plant will flower later than it should. Indeed, at the beginning of the century there was a vogue for pruning half of a mid-season clematis lightly and the remaining vines hard, thus providing flowers right through the summer. In any case, when restoring an overgrown specimen, you may need to cut it back hard and start again.

1 *If left unpruned, this clematis (supported on a framework of twigs) will grow from the top of the previous year's growth, producing small flowers high up from thin wood.*

2 *Remove all the dead wood and then take out the thin vines. Cut down to ground level pieces of main stem that are in the way or unsightly - new growth will soon replace them.*

Clematis that need light pruning

Doubles and
semi-doubles
Early large-flowered
varieties

Right: *'Nelly Moser' is typical of the early large-flowered varieties, and will flower twice in one season if it is lightly pruned.*

3 At this stage, most of the thin and dead wood has gone, leaving the main vines as a framework. Choose the healthiest and strongest ones to ensure good flowering.

You may also like to take out some of the older wood in order to keep the plant young.

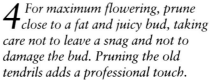

4 For maximum flowering, prune close to a fat and juicy bud, taking care not to leave a snag and not to damage the bud. Pruning the old tendrils adds a professional touch.

5 Add more twigs as needed to support the stems. For clematis growing through a shrub or small tree, you can remove it from its host during pruning and then re-attach it.

Pruning the tendrils

On well-established plants, the old leaf stems can make the finished result look untidy, as well as leading to the possibility of disease gaining entry. Cutting them off may seem a fiddly task, but it certainly enhances the finished appearance of the plant and will help to avoid the onset of any problems. However, be sure to use very sharp secateurs and take your time to avoid making mistakes.

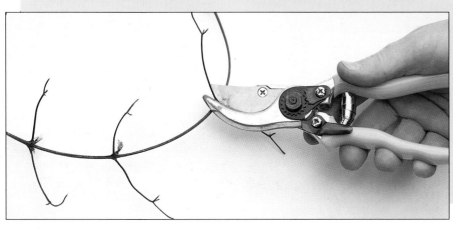

6 Paper-covered wire twist ties are ideal for fastening clematis to a trellis or another plant. One twist is enough - tying them too tightly may cause bruising. Use enough twists to prevent the risk of wind damage and add further ties as the plant grows to encourage flowers in the right places.

Hard pruning

This section includes some of the most useful and rewarding varieties. They produce their flowers on new wood each year, so that the flowers appear progressively higher up the plant unless it is controlled. Hard pruning is the way. However, if the plant is intended to cover an unsightly shed or fence, then do not prune it at all; just allow the plant to cover everything naturally. *Clematis tangutica* is a good variety for this purpose. Late-flowering clematis that grow up and through conifers and shrubs can be tidied up in late fall by pruning away two-thirds of their growth. This allows the conifer or shrub to flourish and avoids the possibility of winter winds detaching the clematis from its anchorage, whipping it around and damaging the emerging buds.

Timing is the important point to bear in mind. If you prune too early, you could encourage premature new growth that is damaged by frost; if you leave it too late, new growth will make it impossible to do the job properly. The optimum time is early spring, when the buds are just beginning to swell. These varieties are also very likely to put up strong basal shoots in early spring, which are highly tempting to slugs and snails. A thin application of slug pellets or a layer of sharp gravel around the base of the plant will control the problem and allow the clematis to flower from top to bottom.

Below: This pruning category includes the herbaceous and semi-herbaceous group of clematis that die down completely for the winter (see pages 34-35). Here, the new shoots are beginning to emerge in the spring.

1 *In some years, your clematis may begin to grow quite early, before you have had the chance to prune it. However, even at this stage, it is not too late to prune it down to some healthy new shoots. Take care not to break these off while you are removing the old wood.*

Clematis that need hard pruning

Herbaceous varieties
Species
Summer hybrids
Texensis and hybrids
Viticellas

2 Hard pruning means exactly that and can be quite severe. This clematis is being pruned almost to ground level in order to encourage strong shoots to appear from below ground.

Remove and compost all the old wood, taking care not to damage the plant supports or parts of the tree or shrub through which the clematis is growing.

Make sure that your secateurs are razor sharp and properly adjusted to avoid leaving snags and jagged edges that could harbor disease.

Below: *A dense growth of* Clematis tangutica, *typical of the species that thrive on hard pruning. You can tidy up such plants for the winter by doing half the pruning and then complete the job in early spring.*

Put down a few slug pellets. Clematis are very vulnerable at this stage.

3 New shoots soon begin to grow after pruning, even from below ground level. At this time, the clematis will benefit from a dressing of well-rotted compost or manure.

Cutting back a montana

The montana, evergreen and alpina groups seldom require pruning; indeed it is often best to allow them to grow unhindered for maximum bloom. However, there may come a time when these plants have either outgrown their allotted space or have become old and uncontrollable, so that some pruning has to be done. The main point to remember is that these plants produce most of their flowers on the previous season's wood, so carry out pruning immediately after flowering to allow the new growth time to mature and form flowerbuds for the next season's show. Pruning can be quite brutal and you can use hedging shears to clear much of the growth, but with the more substantial shoots it does pay to prune back as close as possible to a leaf bud to prevent the risk of dieback. After pruning, apply a general fertilizer and water well.

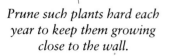

Prune such plants hard each year to keep them growing close to the wall.

Above: *This beautiful display of flowers has been produced by this Clematis montana 'Tetrarose' on the previous year's growth, which was tied securely to the wall immediately after pruning was carried out.*

1 *First, use sharp secateurs to remove the very old, thin or dead wood. This will give you some space to carry out the rest of the pruning.*

2 *Remove any really tangled pieces as you go. If you leave these, they will only get worse and more difficult to sort out the following year.*

3 *It is a good idea to remove some of the older, thicker stems in sections. This avoids damaging the stems you do want to keep and makes working so much easier, especially if you are on a ladder.*

4 *Once you have removed most of the unwanted shoots, tie the remaining ones to their support and then carefully cut away any thin shoots that show up.*

Train these shoots as you wish, allowing room for vigorous growth.

Twisted leaves will soon turn towards the light.

5 *Do not worry if the finished effect looks rather thin; the plant will soon put on growth from these stems and bear masses of flowers the following spring.*

Common diseases

The most important disease to affect clematis is clematis wilt. The mere thought of it striking has deterred many people from growing clematis. Indeed, it is thought that the decline in popularity suffered by clematis in the early part of the nineteenth century was attributable to its susceptibility to clematis wilt. Unfortunately, wilt tends to strike an otherwise healthy plant just as it is about to burst into full flower, leaving it apparently dead. However, if you have planted the clematis correctly all is not lost, because new shoots invariably appear from its base. At this point, you should cut out all the dead or infected shoots and put some slug pellets around the base of the plant. There is no real cure for clematis wilt, but providing you bought the plant from a reputable supplier, it will soon recover. Drenching the plant with a systemic fungicide will ensure that it will regain its health and flower again.

The only other disease to seriously affect clematis is mildew. This unsightly fungus infection is common in late summer after a period of muggy, humid weather, and shows as a white powder on the leaf surface, before eventually turning the leaf brown. It can spread very rapidly, especially among the later flowering varieties, and in severe cases can completely defoliate the affected plant. Thankfully, it is easy to control by spraying with a good fungicide.

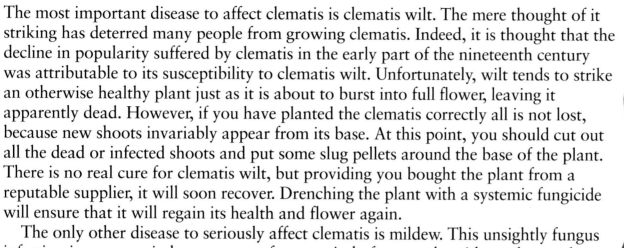

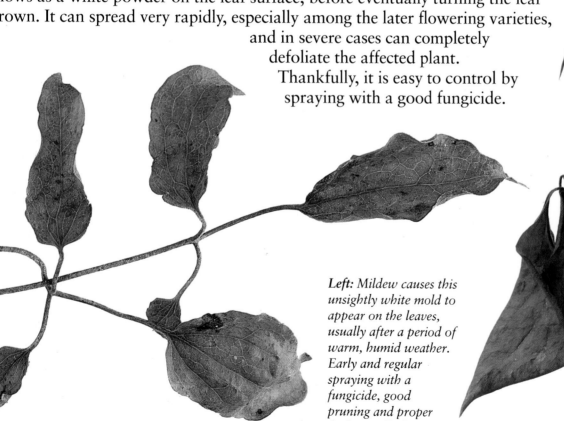

Left: Mildew causes this unsightly white mold to appear on the leaves, usually after a period of warm, humid weather. Early and regular spraying with a fungicide, good pruning and proper feeding will all help to prevent this disease in the first place.

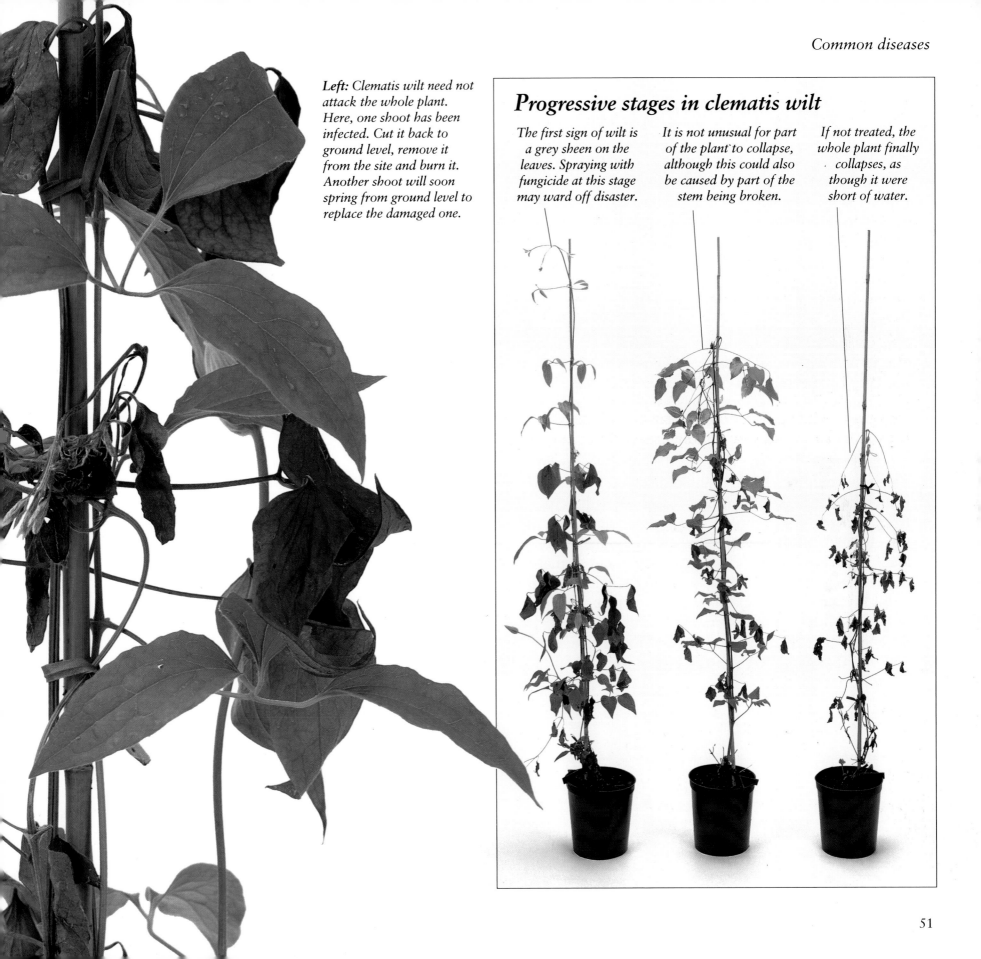

Left: *Clematis wilt need not attack the whole plant. Here, one shoot has been infected. Cut it back to ground level, remove it from the site and burn it. Another shoot will soon spring from ground level to replace the damaged one.*

Progressive stages in clematis wilt

The first sign of wilt is a grey sheen on the leaves. Spraying with fungicide at this stage may ward off disaster.

It is not unusual for part of the plant to collapse, although this could also be caused by part of the stem being broken.

If not treated, the whole plant finally collapses, as though it were short of water.

Common pests

Clematis are not attacked by many pests. The biggest pests are probably slugs and snails, which can cause havoc in moist conditions, eating the new soft shoots as they emerge from ground level and thus preventing the plant from developing a nice bushy habit. People do not always realize that snails can climb to considerable heights in search of succulent shoots and leaves, and can easily prevent a plant from flowering altogether. Earwigs are another potential source of damage to the blooms of your clematis, especially if the plant is growing against a wall. These creatures come out at night and nibble holes in the unopened bud, preventing it from ever becoming a flower. If your clematis is growing in a conservatory or in a very sheltered part of the garden, you may come across leaves that seem to have white lines weaving across them. These are caused by the grub of the leaf miner. This little insect does not do very much damage, but can make the clematis look unsightly. The only other pest is the ubiquitous aphid in all colors from green through pink. These insects suck the sap from your plant and may leave a gummy deposit on the leaves, much loved by ants. Eventually you may find black mold growing on these deposits. If your clematis should seem to be short of water even though you know it cannot be, check the base of the plant for signs of an ants' nest. These insects can tunnel for long distances, increasing the drainage channels in the soil and thus diverting moisture away from the roots.

Earwigs are active at night, and cause the damage shown here. Earwigs not only damage the clematis flowers but can also reduce the leaves to a network of veins.

Right: *This portion of a clematis plant has clearly suffered damage from the attentions of snails and earwigs*

Problems and cures

Slugs and snails: *Put down pellets or scatter sharp grit around the base of the plant to deter these pests.*
Earwigs: *Difficult to control, but you can trap them in an upturned flowerpot filled with newspaper.*
Leaf miner: *Spray with a systemic insecticide early in the season.*

Aphids: *Spray regularly with a good insecticide, preferably one that is specific to aphids and does not harm beneficial insects, such as ladybugs and lacewings.*
Ants: *Scatter ant powder around the base of the plant. Always follow the maker's instructions.*

Below: *Left untreated, aphids can soon build up to large proportions, transmitting virus disease and causing clematis leaves to curl.*

Above: *These are the patterns left in the leaves by larvae eating their way through the soft tissues. Pick off and burn any leaves affected by leaf miners to prevent reinfestation later.*

Below: *Be sure to spray underneath leaves and flowers to control the pests lurking there, such as these aphids. If you do not do this within a day or so, the pests will build up again.*

Aphids attract ants to feed on the honeydew they excrete.

Aphids cluster around the stem and can breed without fertilization. Be sure to spray before heavy infestations like this occur.

These are typical signs of slug and snail damage. These pests are more likely to be a problem during wet summers.

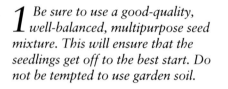

1 *Be sure to use a good-quality, well-balanced, multipurpose seed mixture. This will ensure that the seedlings get off to the best start. Do not be tempted to use garden soil.*

2 *Gently firm the seed mixture and level the surface with the base of another seed tray. This ensures that all the seeds are at the same depth and avoids the risk of erratic germination.*

Growing clematis plants from seed

Growing any plant from seed can be a most rewarding activity, and clematis are generally easy and reliable plants to grow this way. Remember that named varieties will not come true to type and that the species may show marked variations, but this just adds to the excitement. Growing from seed demands very clean conditions and equipment, as any dirt or rotting debris can cause disease and pest infestation, which will stifle the plant at birth. To test the viability of seed, place some in a glass of water and swirl it lightly. The more seeds that float, the less viable the seed. Clematis in general need a period of cold before they will germinate. If you are unable to put the finished seed tray outside during the winter or wish to sow in the spring, you can ensure more rapid germination by placing the seed together with some moist silver sand in a sealed plastic bag and putting this into the refrigerator for a month or two before sowing the whole lot in the usual way.

Buy your seeds from a reputable supplier. Make sure they are fresh or have been stored in cool, dry conditions.

3 *Sprinkle the seeds thinly over the surface of the seed mix, making sure they are evenly spaced and not overcrowded, which can lead to damping-off.*

4 *Use a fine sieve to cover the seeds evenly with more seed mixture and to anchor them in place. Germination will take up to three weeks, depending on the variety and the time of year.*

5 *Once the seeds are covered, water them in gently, using a watering can fitted with a fine rose. Take care not to drown the seeds or wash away the covering layer of seed mixture.*

6 *Label the seed tray and cover it with a thin sheet of plastic to maintain humidity. If you are going to put the tray outside, use fine wire mesh instead of the plastic to keep mice and birds off the seeds.*

7 *When the seedlings have germinated, pot them on into a good-quality potting mixture. Make a suitably sized hole for the seedlings using a piece of bamboo as a dibber.*

8 *Transfer the seedlings gently from the seed tray into small pots. Be sure to hold them by their seed leaves and never by the stem, which can easily bruise and then die back.*

The seed leaves should be just level with the soil surface.

Square plastic pots measuring 2in(5cm) across are ideal for clematis seedlings when they have been pricked out.

9 *Place the clematis seedlings into the potting mix up to the first pair of seed leaves. Gently firm the seedlings in to ensure that their roots are in contact with the potting mix and water well in.*

10 *Label each pot carefully. Once the seedlings are established, they grow rapidly and you can expect a first flush of flowers when the plants are about three or four years old.*

Taking cuttings

This method of propagation is used for many plants. It means you can produce a relatively large number of new plants at once and, unlike propagation from seed, the resulting progeny will all be like the parent plant. However, in the case of clematis, it is not the easiest method, so start with montanas or one of the other vigorous species before going on to the early summer hybrids. The best time to take cuttings is in late spring and early summer, using the soft, new shoots on the current year's growth. Avoid taking cuttings in the heat of the day. If you take cuttings some distance away from where you carry out the final preparation, place them immediately in a plastic bag for transportation. The most important thing to remember when propagating by cuttings - whatever the plant - is to prevent the cuttings from losing water. Remember that until they have formed roots, they cannot pick up any water from the soil. Misting the plants occasionally with a fine spray will help them to retain moisture, as will covering them with plastic. Take care not to overdo this, however, as disease can set in and quickly ruin an otherwise fine batch of cuttings.

4 *If the section of stem between the leaf joints is very long, reduce it so that the cutting will eventually be at the right depth in the potting mixture.*

1 *Select your cutting material from a good healthy plant and take it from the present year's growth. Make sure all your tools are razor sharp and have a bag ready to take the cuttings.*

2 *Place your shoot on a hard firm surface and, using a craft knife, cut the stem just above a pair of buds. The blade and cutting surface must be scrupulously clean to avoid disease.*

3 *You can take a number of cuttings from one shoot, but do make sure you only use the best sections. Be ruthless and discard all the thin, weak parts.*

This piece is too thin and soft and should be discarded.

These sections will make ideal cuttings, as they are firm and healthy pieces of the plant.

6 Dip the cutting into hormone rooting powder. Carefully insert it into a pot containing 50 percent peat and 50 percent grit. Do not add fertilizer at this stage; in fact, it can inhibit rooting.

Do not leave the cuttings like this for long or they will lose water.

Hormone rooting powder

5 Some clematis varieties have large leaves, so to reduce the water loss from your cutting, remove part or all of one leaf. If the cuttings are smaller, you can put more of them in each pot.

7 Cuttings root best when inserted around the edge of the pot. At this stage it is vital to give them a thorough watering.

8 Cover the pot with a plastic bag to retain a humid atmosphere and place the pot out of direct sunlight. The cuttings should root within three to four weeks and can then be potted up.

Turn the bag inside out occasionally to prevent the buildup of excessive condensation, which can cause disease to set in.

57

Propagation by layering

Layering is probably the easiest and most reliable way of propagating clematis. Not only is it almost bound to succeed, but the resulting plant will be exactly the same as its parent. The usual time for layering is in late spring or early summer, but it will even work during the winter months, providing the soil is not too cold or wet. Select a healthy shoot, with no trace of pest or disease damage. Some gardeners recommend making a small cut below the leaf joint to promote more rapid rooting. This is fine if the shoot is thick enough, but in most cases you will find that it roots without this. If your soil is less than ideal, it is probably best to put the shoot into a pot or small seed tray. This also means that you need not wait until the winter when the plant is dormant to move it to its new position. Rooting tends to take up to three months and if it is successful, a new shoot emerges from the point where the leaf joint was buried. At this stage, the biggest danger is slug damage or knocking the plant accidentally while hoeing. Insert a small cane and tie the shoot to it to make it more visible, and scatter a few slug pellets around it. After rooting and before moving your new plant, cut the original stem just before the new shoot, carefully lift the new clematis without damaging the roots and pot it up into a good-quality potting mix. Allow it time to establish itself before planting it in its new position. It will then grow rapidly and your clematis should flower the following year.

1 Select a strong, disease-free shoot and separate it from the parent plant. It is vital to select a leaf joint with strong buds showing, as these will eventually form the new plant.

Make sure your secateurs are sharp, as bruising or jagged edges can lead to disease.

2 Carefully remove the leaves, making a clean cut as close as possible to the main stem. Take care not to damage the buds lying in the joints where the stem and leaves meet.

3 Using a trowel, make a hole about 1in(2.5cm) deep in which to place the shoot. Sprinkle a little silver sand into the planting hole to aid drainage and prevent rotting.

4 Place the layer onto the surface of the soil with the buds over the hole you have already made. Put a little sharp sand in the bottom of the hole so that the buds do not get too wet.

5 Bend pieces of garden wire about 3in(7.5cm) long into a U-shape and insert them in the soil on either side of the buds to prevent your layer being dislodged by wind.

6 Make sure that you press the wires in firmly so that the leaf joint is directly in contact with the soil. This should prevent it from drying out during the summer months.

7 As an extra security measure, place some stones on either side to anchor your layer. These will also act as a marker later on.

8 Cover the buds with soil or potting mix so that the surface is level. Firm down gently. Water lightly if the soil is on the dry side.

9 The layer will take three or four months before shoots emerge. During this time ensure that the soil does not dry out and protect with slug pellets during the summer months.

A split cane placed here will help mark your layer and provide support for the new shoots.

1 Select two clematis varieties with different characteristics. Ensure that the flowers have not been pollinated and that both the male and female parts have not been damaged.

Breeding a new hybrid clematis

There are several hundred clematis hybrids available today, many of which have arisen by chance after a batch of seedlings have been allowed to flower. Many of the best ones have been planned, and this is not as complicated as you may at first imagine. The process involves selecting two clematis, each with different characteristics, but which flower at the same time. One is treated as the male partner, the other as the female. After fertilization by the male's pollen, the female will eventually set seed and the resultant offspring should inherit some of its parents' characteristics. This may be color, size of flower or a range of other quirks that you may wish to see in a plant. There are many goals to aim for; for example, there is not yet a really good large-flowered yellow clematis, nor is there a red *tangutica* variety and yet both these possibilities are feasible. Although it is not a project that yields results overnight, the excitement you feel when the first flowers appear on your 'new' hybrid clematis makes the hard work worthwhile - and of course you can take great pride in naming it.

Use tweezers to carry out the more delicate operations. Take care not to damage the parts of the flower you wish to use.

2 This plant has been selected as the female. To avoid self-pollination, carefully remove the male parts, or anthers, leaving only the female parts, which will eventually form seed.

New combinations

There are a number of gaps waiting to be filled in the clematis world. Here, C. flammula, *a very scented variety, is to be crossed with* Clematis 'Niobe', *in the hope of obtaining a large-flowered scented red variety. It may take several attempts, using the progeny of the original crosses, to achieve the desired results.*

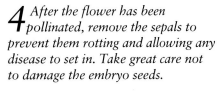

Use a paper bag and not a plastic one. Plastic heats the flower and can cause disease to set in.

3 To transfer the pollen from the male flower to the female flower, simply brush the two together. The best time to do this is around midday, when the pollen is most viable.

4 After the flower has been pollinated, remove the sepals to prevent them rotting and allowing any disease to set in. Take great care not to damage the embryo seeds.

5 Cover the flowerhead with a paper bag so that there is no chance of a bee or other insect reaching the plant and depositing stray pollen from another variety.

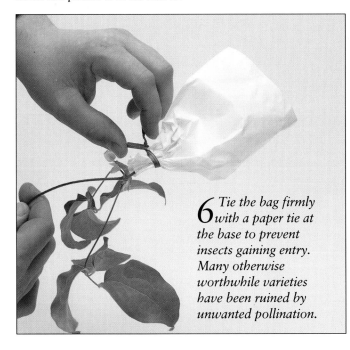

6 Tie the bag firmly with a paper tie at the base to prevent insects gaining entry. Many otherwise worthwhile varieties have been ruined by unwanted pollination.

This is the seedhead of a hybrid clematis that has been successfully pollinated.

This seedhead is from a species clematis that has been successfully pollinated.

A badly fertilized seedhead. Only a few seeds have set and these may not be viable.

This sterile and unfertilized seedhead will not set seed and should be discarded.

Part Two

USING AND ENJOYING CLEMATIS

Clematis are such versatile and amenable plants that you can pick a variety for almost any situation. In the garden, there are cultivars for every aspect of walls, pergolas and trellis screens, and many are hardy enough to withstand the most inhospitable conditions. Some types are best suited to scrambling through a tree or shrub, whereas others are more valuable cascading in garlands of blooms as a specimen plant. There are compact, free-flowering clematis that make absolutely stunning subjects for a container on a terrace or patio, and there are species clematis that will smother an ugly fence or shed in one season. There are so many ways of training clematis in the garden, that it is possible to create almost any shape and density with a little ingenuity. Many cultivars and species can be accommodated within the garden border and become very useful for filling awkward spaces, improving the continuity of a border color scheme or increasing the flowering period of a particular area of the garden. In a cold greenhouse or conservatory, some of the less hardy or more easily wind-damaged types will make a spectacular pot plant and many of these have the added bonus of a delightful scent, often in the gloomy winter and early spring months. Even in the house, the cut blooms last well in water and so clematis can be used in flower arranging, their colors mingling sympathetically with other flowers and foliage. And even once the flowering season is over, the seedheads can make a valuable contribution to fall and early winter decorations. With so many ideas to choose from, the biggest problem is knowing when to stop.

*Left: 'Huldine' and 'Ernest Markham' planted together. **Right:** A potted clematis ready to grow.*

Clematis for sunny places

Although clematis in general require cool, moist soil in which to spread their roots, this does not mean that you cannot grow them in full sun. Indeed, many varieties, especially the doubles, require the warming influence of the summer sun to ripen their wood and prepare the following year's buds. Some single varieties also need this warmth to thrive and do not do at all well in summers when sunlight is lacking. Providing you are able to give your clematis all the water and food they require, there are many varieties to choose from. As well as the double varieties, the deeper-colored hybrids are very well suited to a sunny position. Placing a large stone or, perhaps, a small, silver-leaved plant at the base helps to retain moisture in the soil, thus reducing the need to water to some extent. Clematis grown in a sunny spot tend not to suffer from mildew quite so much, but their lower leaves may turn brown and be shed much earlier. Indeed, varieties such as 'Ville de Lyon' can lose nearly threequarters of their leaves by the end of summer, but this does not matter if you plant your clematis to grow through other plants to disguise this feature.

Left: *The deep red flowers of Clematis 'Madame Edouard André', with their cream stamens, have more than enough color to cope with even the sunniest position in the garden.*

Above: *The vigorous and prolifically flowered Clematis 'Jackmanii Superba' is rewarding in any position, but performs exceptionally well in sun and is ideal for arches and pergolas.*

Above: *The pearly white flowers of Clematis 'Huldine' are superb in late summer. Here it is growing through an apple tree, whose fruits will provide another contrast.*

Left: *The natural tendency of 'Ville de Lyon' to lose its lower leaves is more pronounced when it is grown in sun. Grow it through another shrub to hide the base of the stem.*

Clematis for sun

Clematis armandii,
C. cirrhosa,
'Beauty of Worcester', 'Huldine',
'Lady Northcliffe', 'Proteus',
'Royalty', 'Ville de Lyon'
'Vyvyan Pennell'
C. florida 'Alba Plena',
C. florida 'Sieboldii'

Below: The large and spectacular blooms of the well-known clematis 'Nelly Moser' are even more colorful, and keep their color longer, when the plant is out of the glare of full sun.

Clematis for shady places

It is not always appreciated that, given the right growing conditions, all clematis will grow perfectly well in quite shady positions. The main problems that can affect a clematis grown in shade are concerned with the plant's ability to produce flowers and the coloration of those flowers. The double hybrids, for example, need a certain amount of sun and warmth if they are to produce the buds that will produce double flowers the following year. Growing these varieties in shade often means that you will only get the later, single flowers. Clematis growing in a sunless spot sometimes fail to produce any color pigment, with the result that the flowers appear to be green. Even this is not a disadvantage if you happen to be a flower arranger. Bear in mind that the scented varieties of clematis depend on the warmth of the sun to produce the pungent aromatic oils that give them their perfume. Even though they may grow and flower perfectly well, they release no scent. However, some clematis benefit from a degree of shade. 'Nelly Moser', for example, when planted in full sun quickly fades to a dirty gray color. Indeed, most of the lighter-colored, large-flowered hybrids require less sunlight to maintain their full depth of color.

Right: Most large-flowered hybrids grow very successfully when planted in shade. The absence of sunlight usually means that they have the cool, moist root run that they prefer.

Below: With their distinctive creamy centers, the prolific mauve flowers of Clematis 'Barbara Jackman' will brighten up a shady corner in the garden during early summer.

Below: *The semi-herbaceous variety* Clematis x eriostemon *'Hendersonii' was the first hybrid clematis to be produced. It is still a fine variety, especially in a shady spot.*

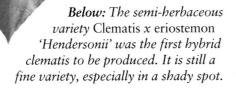

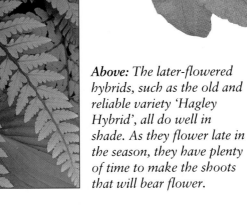

Above: *The later-flowered hybrids, such as the old and reliable variety 'Hagley Hybrid', all do well in shade. As they flower late in the season, they have plenty of time to make the shoots that will bear flower.*

Clematis for shade

C. alpina *'Francis Rivis'*,
C.a. *'Ruby'*,
C. x eriostemon *'Hendersonii'*
C. *macropetala*,
C.m. *'Markham's Pink'*,
C. montana *and its varieties*
C. viticella *and its varieties'*
'Barbara Jackman',
'Nelly Moser', *'Hagley Hybrid'*

Scented clematis for the garden

Scent adds another dimension to any plant. Unfortunately, there are only a few clematis varieties that possess this characteristic and most of them require a warm climate and a clear nose. The pale pink varieties of *Clematis montana*, particularly *C.m.* 'Elizabeth', are among the most reliable, releasing a vanilla perfume that is carried on the air on warm spring evenings. Later in the summer, the vigorous European species, *Clematis flammula*, comes into its own. Again, the scent is of vanilla and on a balmy summer evening this can fill the entire garden.

As far as the plant is concerned, the purpose of scent is to attract the insects that will carry out the pollination process. The late-flowering *C. recta* fulfils this function almost to excess. Its heavy, sweet scent attracts a multitude of colorful butterflies and the beneficial hoverflies, whose larvae devour aphids in vast numbers. Sadly, there is an absence of scent within the large-flowered varieties. *Clematis* 'Fair Rosamond', an otherwise undistinguished white variety, is reputed to have the scent of violets, but it is not easy to detect.

Although not reliably hardy, the New Zealand species *Clematis forsteri* is worth considering. Given the protection and warmth of a cold greenhouse or conservatory, this greenish yellow-flowered species produces a mass of flowers with a fresh citrus scent. This clematis is usually produced from seed and the amount of perfume does vary from plant to plant, so choose a reliably scented form.

Right: Clematis flammula *is one of the most perfumed varieties. Masses of small, white starlike flowers are produced during the late summer and release a lovely vanilla scent.*

Right: As well as sweetly scented flowers in summer, the herbaceous Clematis heracleifolia davidiana *has aromatic dry foliage in the fall.*

Scented clematis

C. armandii, C.a. 'Snowdrift',
C.a. 'Apple Blossom',
C. flammula,
C. forsteri,
C. heracleifolia davidiana,
C. recta, C. rehderiana,
C. *x* triternata 'Rubra
Marginata',
'Fair Rosamond'

Right: *A well-grown specimen of Clematis montana 'Elizabeth' will provide such an abundance of fragrant flowers that your spring garden will be filled with its perfume.*

Below: *The evergreen species Clematis armandii and its various named forms produce clusters of sweetly scented flowers during the spring.*

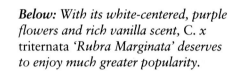

Below: *With its white-centered, purple flowers and rich vanilla scent, C. x triternata 'Rubra Marginata' deserves to enjoy much greater popularity.*

Clematis on walls

Walls are often regarded as the ideal place to grow climbing plants, and clematis have been the first choice for many years. To succeed, it is vital to carry out the initial planting correctly. The base of a wall can be a very dry and inhospitable place and because clematis require more water than the average plant, they often fail when planted in this position, even during the wettest season. It is a good idea to plant the clematis about 12-18in (30-45cm) away from the base of the wall and to incorporate plenty of water-retaining material, such as peat. From early spring and right through the growing period, make sure the clematis does not go short of water. Another important consideration is a means of supporting the clematis. There is a wide range of plant supports on the market and your choice is only a matter of personal taste. Alternatively, you can support the clematis with another climber or shrub. This is also a good way of providing protection in winter for a more delicate clematis, such as *Clematis florida* 'Sieboldii', and makes a foil for the flowers.

Above: *Make an unobtrusive support by stretching galvanized wire between lead-headed wall nails or wire eyes. Space the wires about 24in(60cm) apart and loosely tie in the clematis with paper-covered wire ties. The support and clematis will not damage a wall in good condition.*

Left: *Square mesh wire is normally used to enclose animals, but here it is providing a support for the clematis 'Daniel Deronda'. You can attach the wire mesh to the wall with lead-headed wall nails.*

Trellis for clematis

Hardwood trellis makes a good support for clematis and is widely available in many styles and colors. Clematis need room to attach themselves by their leaf stems, so space the trellis 0.5in (1.25cm) away from the wall with pieces of bamboo. Secure the trellis with masonry nails.

Above: *A narrow section of hardwood trellis is ideal where space is limited. Grow a compact clematis, such as the 'Comtesse de Bouchaud' shown here.*

Left: *Hardwood trellis can also be used horizontally. The line of the trellis should follow that of the bricks, otherwise it looks odd in winter.*

Below: *If space allows, use a wider section of trellis and choose a more vigorous clematis or grow more than one variety. Spread out the stems as they grow .*

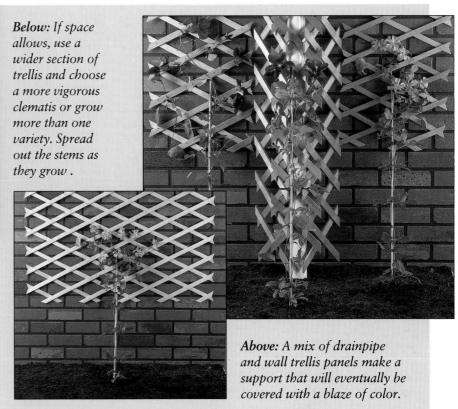

Above: *A mix of drainpipe and wall trellis panels make a support that will eventually be covered with a blaze of color.*

Right: *A clematis will grow just as well horizontally. Here, Clematis 'Rouge Cardinal' is trained on plastic mesh. The hard pruning it gets each year encourages it to flower low down.*

Clematis for walls

Clematis alpina *'Ruby'*
C. a. *'Burford White'*
Clematis armandii
Clematis cirrhosa
Clematis florida *'Sieboldii'*
Clematis viticella *'Etoile Violette'*
'Comtesse de Bouchaud'
'Daniel Deronda'
'Marie Boisselot'
'Nelly Moser'
'Rouge Cardinal'

Growing on drainpipes

Some of the most unsightly structures on a house are often the drainpipes on the walls. Here clematis come into their own, because with the right supports, these plants can turn an unsightly pipe into a colorful feature. Bear in mind that if the drainpipe is made of metal you cannot attach the plant directly to it, as metal pipes are subject to considerable temperature variations, which plants detest. However, clematis do need something to cling to, so the system illustrated here is ideal. It not only provides the necessary support for the plant, but also holds the plant away from the pipe. The structure is easy to move if you need to maintain the pipe and also looks quite decorative on its own during the winter when the clematis is dormant. The type of clematis you grow is a matter of personal taste and the aspect of the house. If you choose a late-flowering hybrid you can prune it down quite severely for the winter to keep it tidy. The main problem may well be lack of planting space, but in this case you can plant the clematis in a container. As long as you feed and water the clematis regularly, it will thrive for many years.

1 This type of hardwood support is designed to fit around a drainpipe and is readily available and very easy to assemble. Start by laying out the three trellis panels side-by-side.

5 Move the assembled support carefully and place it around the drainpipe and against the wall. When you are happy with the position, fix it firmly to the pipe with plastic ties.

2 The three trellis sections are the same but by sliding one slightly forward of the other and creating an angle between them you will be able to interlock the edges securely.

3 Hold the middle section as you interlock the edges of the third piece. The result is a three-sided structure that, even at this stage, is rigid enough to support itself.

4 Before offering the trellis up to the pipe, it is a good idea to stretch a couple of rubber bands across the protruding edges of the panels to hold the pieces together as you move it.

6 Dig a generous hole and prepare the soil in the base before lowering the clematis into it. Position the plant about 18in(45cm) away from the wall in line with or to one side of the pipe.

Suitable clematis

Clematis alpina 'Columbine'
C. a. 'Burford White'
Clematis macropetala
Clematis viticella 'Minuet'
C. v. 'Royal Velours'
'Comtesse de Bouchaud'
'Nelly Moser'
'Niobe'
'The President'
'Vyvyan Pennell'

7 Hold the bamboo cane to support the plant and carefully replace the soil around the roots. Make sure that the rootball is at least 3in(7.5cm) below the level in the original pot.

8 To begin with, you can guide the clematis into the support by attaching the original bamboo cane to the trellis. As the shoots grow, tie them in carefully with twist ties.

9 The clematis will soon grow and cover the trellis support, but do remember that the base of walls can be very dry and you must feed and water the plants well for good results.

Free-standing trellis and plant supports

For many years, roses have been grown as pillars in gardens, but clematis can also be used to great effect in this way, creating a colorful exclamation mark in the border and providing useful height. You can use a simple, rustic pole and grow a variety such as *Clematis* 'Jackmanii Superba' to great effect or, if you prefer, you could choose one of the many interesting plant supports now available, which are decorative in their own right. Many of the early summer, large-flowered hybrids flourish very well when grown in this way, but they require light pruning. The later-flowering clematis may prove a better option, as they are cut back hard in early spring, which allows you to train the new growth easily to achieve the desired effect. Varieties such as *Clematis* 'Margot Koster' have sufficient vigor to produce a fine display of flowers year after year, and will tolerate either a sunny or shady position without ill-effect. Clematis can also be grown very effectively to make what Victorian gardeners called a 'fedge' - a cross between a fence and a hedge formed by growing a climbing plant, such as *C. montana* 'Rubens', up and through a fence made of galvanized or plastic-coated wire mesh. It eventually makes an impenetrable barrier packed with color. This is an excellent garden feature that is cheap to create and easy to control by clipping back after flowering.

Above: The bright red viticella hybrid 'Madame Julia Correvon' holds its flowers well away from the foliage, making it ideal for growing as a pillar.

Left: A free-standing plant support constructed from flexible hardwood strips. Growing through it is C. viticella 'Alba Luxurians', which after pruning will quickly grow to festoon the support with white bell flowers in late summer.

Right: This is the plant support shown on the opposite page clothed with C. viticella 'Margot Koster', which makes all its growth and flower during the current year. An annual hard prune will ensure a good show every year.

The mauve-pink flowers of Clematis 'Victoria' will tolerate a sunny position, although they will eventually fade in strong sun, but this is quite a pleasant feature.

Below: A simple section of trellis can become a stunning feature when clothed with a clematis in full bloom. This is 'Victoria', a late-flowering hybrid that will thrive a plant support.

Left: *Plant supports such as this one are ideal for growing clematis on. They are decorative even in the winter and early spring before the clematis has begun to show. It is made of hardwood, so give it an occasional wipe with teak oil to keep it in prime condition.*

Arches and pergolas

There is a huge range of arches and pergolas to choose from and they can become one of the most decorative features of the garden. Clematis are ideal for clothing these structures. Their masses of flowers and growth habit, whether they are grown alone or in conjunction with other plants, means that you can enjoy a colorful feature for most of the year. The vigor of *Clematis tangutica* or *C. orientalis* will cover even a quite sizeable pergola very quickly, and the mass of small, yellow, lantern flowers followed by fluffy seedheads will give a dazzling show in late summer. The more compact growing hybrids, including *Clematis* 'Royalty' and 'Lady Northcliffe', are best grown in association with another plant, such as roses, while the late summer and viticella hybrids look superb when used to cover an arch. Although it is tempting to use more than one variety to provide a continuous flowering period through the summer or just for decorative appeal, generally speaking an arch covered with just one variety, say *Clematis* 'Jackmanii Superba', will be far more dramatic and eye-catching. Scented varieties of clematis, such as *C. flammula*, are ideal for pergolas, where you can linger and enjoy the flowers and their perfume.

Above: Clematis 'Hagley Hybrid' and the fragrant evergreen honeysuckle Lonicera japonica 'Halliana' combine effectively over a cottage door. Give the clematis a light prune in spring.

Right: Late-flowering hybrids are ideal for growing up and through arches. Hard prune, then loosely tie in the growing shoots so that they cover the structure.

Left: *Pergolas and arches are generally sighted in sunny positions. Choose the deeper-colored varieties of clematis to cover them to avoid the inevitable fading that affects the lighter varieties when they are planted in full sun.*

Above: Clematis tangutica *is so vigorous that it easily covers even a large pergola, producing a cascade of flowers in late summer. Leave it unpruned for complete cover.*

Left: Clematis 'Perle d'Azur' *is without doubt the best late-flowered blue variety and vigorous enough to grow with honeysuckle to form a colorful and fragrant arch.*

Suitable clematis

Clematis flammula
Clematis montana 'Elizabeth'
C. m. 'Vera'
Clematis orientalis 'Bill Mackenzie'
Clematis tangutica
Clematis viticella
C. v. 'Abundance'
C. v. 'Etoile Violette'
'Gipsy Queen'
'Jackmanii Superba'

Clematis in trees

In common with many other climbing shrubs, clematis are naturally suited to growing through trees. However, you need to choose the most appropriate tree, bearing in mind that not all trees are suitable host subjects. For example, it would be difficult if not impossible to grow even the most vigorous montana variety through a beech tree, as the tree's roots take up so much water that the clematis would never establish itself. However, most of the small decorative trees and fruit trees planted in modern gardens are perfectly satisfactory, providing you observe a few basic rules. For the best results, plant the clematis at the edge of the tree's canopy, leading the shoots into the branches with some strong string.

This ensures that the clematis is not immediately under pressure from the roots of the host tree. Whenever possible, plant it on the side of the tree trunk that does not receive the midday sun, i.e. the side more likely to be cool and moist. Choose a clematis variety that reflects the vigor of the host tree. Generally speaking, the montana, viticella and species groups are the most suitable. Consider the flowering times of both the clematis and the tree. A common mistake is to grow a montana through an apple tree, but as both bear similar flowers at the same time, there is not much to be gained from this. It would be much more effective to plant a *tangutica* and enjoy its flowers and seedheads later in the year. As this variety requires hard pruning, you can remove most of the growth before pruning the apple tree, which makes pruning the tree easier, and then cut down the rest of the clematis later on.

Above: A vigorous montana can cope happily with growing through a tree. It can even be pruned and trained to create a more delicate effect.

Left: Viticella hybrids and conifers associate well. Here C.v. 'Abundance' scrambles through Juniperus 'Skyrocket'.

Right: *The contrast between the long racemes of yellow laburnum flowers and the pale pink clusters of* Clematis montana *'Elizabeth' provide a vibrant festival of color in the spring and the scent of the clematis will fill the air.*

Clematis for trees

C. flammula
C. montana, C. m. *'Elizabeth'*
C. m. *'Tetrarose'*
C. orientalis *'Bill Mackenzie'*
C. rehderiana, C. tangutica
C. *x* triternata
'Rubra Marginata'
C. viticella *'Alba Luxurians'*
C. v. *'Purpurea Plena Elegans'*

Left: *By growing clematis through trees, the sunlight is able to play on the flowers, making the colors far more vibrant. Shadows from the branches and leaves passing over the flowers add another dimension.*

Below: *The vigor of the montana group of clematis makes them highly suitable for growing up and through quite large leaves, creating a riot of color and fragrance during the early part of the year.*

The shell pink flowers of 'Comtesse de Bouchaud' become almost translucent in sunlight.

Clematis through tall shrubs

The natural habit of clematis, even when growing strongly, is to be bare at the base, while flowering at the top. However, when grown through a tall shrub, the leggy base is hidden and the full growth and blooms can be appreciated. Clematis can be grown to great effect through some of the spring-flowering shrubs, such as deutzias and forsythias, which can be quite boring for the rest of the year. Choose late-flowering types, such as viticellas, that not only give a display at a difficult time of year for flowers, but can also be hard pruned in time for their host's flowering. Where a planting scheme requires some extra impact, the early large-flowered varieties come into their own. In general, their slighter growth habit makes them compatible with smaller hosts, such as bush roses, and as they only need minimal pruning they are easier to grow through a thorny subject. Clematis are often planted with rambler roses, but try 'Jackmanii Superba' through Virginia creeper, a montana tumbling down a conifer hedge or maybe 'Perle d'Azur' hosted by *Eucalyptus gunnii*. The possibilities are endless, limited only by your imagination.

Right: The crimson flowers of Clematis viticella *'Abundance' and the cream-edged leaves of weigela add color to the late summer garden. The weigela's pink flowers provide the early show.*

Right: *In common with most of the late-flowering hybrids, 'Ville de Lyon' becomes very bare at the base as the season progresses. Growing it through a taller shrub, such as honeysuckle, disguises this feature, while showing off the flowers to perfection. The honeysuckle also provides sweet scent.*

Below: *The late-flowering hybrids are also ideal for growing through roses. The clematis require hard pruning, which makes the job of pruning the roses much easier. Here, Clematis 'Perle d'Azur' complements the pink climbing rose 'Bantry Bay'.*

Suitable clematis

'Bees Jubilee'
Clematis alpina 'Rosy Pagoda'
Clematis macropetala
Clematis viticella 'Abundance'
C.v. 'Alba Luxurians'
C.v. 'Purpurea Plena Elegans'
'Comtesse de Bouchaud'
'Jackmanii Superba'
'Perle d'Azur', 'Ville de Lyon'

Below: *The common golden privet is often overlooked as a shrub. Here, it provides a wonderful golden foil for the deep blue bells of Clematis macropetala. Both will tolerate a degree of shade without ill-effect.*

Clematis through low shrubs

Low-growing shrubs make ideal hosts for a wide variety of clematis, providing an extension of the flowering period or an extra contrast. The texensis hybrids are superb when grown through and over winter-flowering heathers. Their tulip-shaped flowers appear in late summer, and after flowering you can cut them back to allow the winter heathers to come into their own. Carry out the final clematis pruning in early spring, when you give the heathers their 'haircut'. However, mice can make their winter home in heathers and seriously damage the clematis, so place a 12in(30cm) land drain over the base of the plant through which it can grow. It also gives the clematis some height before it tumbles over the heather bed. The late-flowering hybrids and viticellas are also excellent choices. Train some sections of clematis through the shrubs and peg other stems to the ground to provide color at the base. *Clematis viticella* 'Venosa Violacea' holds up its flowers and does not produce too much luxuriant foliage that could swamp a smaller shrub. For this reason, do not use montanas or the more rampant species with low shrubs. Early summer hybrids also work well. With careful training and light pruning, you can have color in the garden for a long period.

Right: *The long stems of* Clematis viticella *'Purpurea Plena Elegans' are wreathed in double mauve flowers in late summer. These contrast well against the silvery foliage of santolina.*

Below left: *A pale pink hybrid* Clematis texensis *'Sir Trevor Lawrence' planted through a low-growing cotoneaster. You can look down into the lovely tulip-shaped clematis flowers.*

Below: The dusky red flowers of Clematis 'Voluceau' are a welcome addition to the late summer garden and provide splashes of color amid the yellow foliage of the beautiful shrub Choisya ternata 'Sundance'.

Arrange the individual stems of the clematis to create the best effect. Secure the stems to the host plant with paper-covered twist ties.

Above: The late-summer hybrid 'Rouge Cardinal' is a trouble-free, rewarding variety. It produces deep red blooms that associate particularly well with heathers, as they do here.

Clematis as ground cover

Until fairly recently, it was rare to see a clematis growing along the ground, although their wiry stems make them well suited to this purpose. However, with the exception of the truly vigorous varieties, most clematis will not smother weeds efficiently and so are best grown in conjunction with other plants that will also provide some support. Nothing could be more stunning than a cascade of montana or tangutica on banks and slopes, but first mulch the ground heavily to discourage weeds. In smaller areas and in borders, choose the early large-flowered varieties. Their large flat flowers can be seen so much better when they look up at you, rather than when they are grown against a wall. Where the clematis is growing over a host plant to provide an extra season of color or to accentuate a scheme, choose the variety carefully. For example, winter-flowering heathers are a boon during the dull months, but tend to look dull in summer. If you select a late summer-flowering clematis, it will require hard pruning, which means that by cutting it back in late summer, after it has flowered, no harm is done to the heathers and they are visible when their blooms are on show. On the other hand, if the clematis is growing through a spiny shrub, such as a ground cover rose, the prudent gardener will select a variety that requires little or no pruning in order to reduce personal suffering! Plant ground cover clematis as you would any other type, paying special attention to soil preparation. If the base of the plant is under other shrubs, slip a piece of drainpipe or a plastic bottle with both ends cut off over the clematis and sink it into the soil. This prevents slugs and mice nibbling at the young shoots and reminds you where you planted it. This is very important in winter, when little growth might be visible. To train the stems, peg them down individually with pieces of bent wire or, for a more solid effect, pin them to a sheet of chicken wire over the soil. Old wire is better, as it is duller and shows up less.

Clematis for cover

C. montana, C.m. 'Elizabeth'
C. m. 'Rubens'
C. viticella 'Abundance'
C. v. 'Etoile Violette'
'H.F. Young'
'Kathleen Wheeler'
'Lincoln Star'
'Niobe'
'Rouge Cardinal'

Below: Clematis 'H.F. Young', an early large-flowered hybrid, is a compact-growing variety that can be used to great effect as ground cover.

The blue flowers of 'H.F. Young' stand away from the foliage to face the sun.

Above: *The later-flowering hybrids are superb plants to use as ground cover. Masses of flowers guarantee a riot of color from midsummer until the first frosts of the fall.*

Left: *Clematis x jouiniana 'Praecox' is one of the true ground-covering clematis. Although not a particularly spectacular plant, it is nevertheless a useful addition to a woodland garden.*

Growing clematis in conservatories

The rise in popularity of conservatories has resulted in the availability of a range of suitable plants. Clematis are eminently suited to growing in a conservatory and this allows you to experiment with some of the less hardy varieties. Some of the more common varieties usually grown outside also make good conservatory plants. The early large-flowered hybrids, such as 'Barbara Jackman', will flower a month or so earlier than normal, while the spectacular blooms of *Clematis florida* 'Sieboldii' can continue well into the winter. The winter-flowering *Clematis cirrhosa* and its varieties do well outside, but never flower so successfully in colder latitudes. In a conservatory they provide an abundance of pale yellow flowers, some with deep red markings, that provide color during the cheerless winter months. Bear in mind that pests and diseases can flourish in conservatories, so inspect your plants regularly and apply any relevant treatments.

Above: When grown in the protected environment of a conservatory, varieties such as 'Bees Jubilee' will flower much earlier than usual, but provide them with some shade or their blooms will fade to a dingy white.

Left: Clematis x cartmanii 'Joe' is a relative newcomer from New Zealand. It is not completely hardy outdoors in temperate climates but grown within a conservatory, it will produce a mass of white flowers.

Suitable clematis

Clematis x cartmanii 'Joe'
Clematis cirrhosa
C. c. balearica
C. c. 'Freckles'
Clematis florida 'Sieboldii'
C. f. 'Alba Plena'
Clematis forsteri
'Comtesse de Bouchaud'
'H.F. Young', 'Lasurstern'

Left: *Conservatories are marvelous places to grow plants, but it is vital to keep them scrupulously clean, as a variety of pests and diseases are likely to flourish in the warm, humid conditions that prevail there.*

Below: Clematis 'Lasurstern' produces pure blue flowers for most of the summer. If the plant is grown in a container, you can move it outside for the winter and replace it with another variety that will flower at this time.

1 Choose a well-balanced potting mixture that will sustain the clematis for a number of years. These are available from garden centers and nurseries.

Planting a clematis in a pot

Planting up a clematis in a pot is somewhat different from planting one in the open ground. The most important difference is the choice of potting mixture. It is often tempting to use soil from the garden, but this invariably leads to poor results. To be certain of success, you must use a good-quality potting mixture that has been specially designed for growing plants in pots. This will contain the correct proportion of materials to allow sufficient air for the roots to breathe and for excess water to drain away. Furthermore, the balanced fertilizer in it will get the plant off to a good start. The type of pot is not particularly important. Clematis will grow equally well in a clay or plastic pot, but whichever you choose, make sure it is spacious. For example, a pot 18in(45cm) across will hold sufficient mixture to sustain the plant's growth over four or five years. With a peat-based mixture, there is no need to place crocks in the bottom of the pot for drainage, so just put a few handfuls of potting mix in the pot and then position the clematis so that the mixture will eventually cover two or three buds. Continue to fill the pot, firming the soil gently to ensure that there is good contact with the rootball, until the surface is about an inch(2.5cm) from the pot's rim. At this point, water the plant until the excess moisture drains out of the base of the pot. If you have chosen a clay pot, remember that because it is porous, it will initially take up a lot of water, so repeat the watering the next day, even if the potting mix seems wet. Three or four weeks after potting up, give the clematis frequent feeds of a tomato fertilizer to ensure that it grows strongly and flowers profusely.

2 Place the clematis onto a layer of potting mixture in the base of the pot, ensuring that the plant will be at the correct depth.

3 Fill the container with the mixture, distributing it evenly around the rootball. Support the plant carefully as you fill the pot.

4 Gently firm the potting mixture as you fill the pot, so that there are no air gaps around the roots. Take care not to damage the clematis stems with your hands as you do this.

5 Continue filling with potting mixture and firming gently until the soil is about 1in(2.5cm) from the rim of the pot.

7 Now you can remove the bamboo cane that supported the plant when you bought it. Arrange the stems against the support and tie them loosely with paper-covered twist ties.

6 Having chosen a suitable support system for the clematis, put it in the pot, taking care not to damage the plant's rootball as you insert the posts around the edge of the container.

8 Water in thoroughly until excess water drains from the base of the pot. Clay pots initially take up a great deal of water.

9 Place the clematis in its final position. You can stand the pot on small 'feet' to improve the drainage. Keep it well-watered and fed during the summer to ensure good flowering.

1 *Place your container in position. Put in a layer of crocks or stones to improve the drainage and fill it with a good-quality, well-balanced potting mixture. Do not use garden soil.*

A support is essential for the clematis to climb up.

Clematis in a wooden trough

Few gardeners realize the value of clematis as a container-grown plant, but in fact they are remarkably versatile, for a space in the border, as a patio plant, to provide welcome color early in the year or for a conservatory or cold greenhouse. There may be occasions when you would like to grow a clematis against a wall, but there is no border in which to plant it. A suitable container will answer this problem. Here we have used a wooden trough with an integral support, but you can use any suitable container and support system. You can grow a clematis like this in most locations and even move it when decoration or repairs are necessary. As long as it is not too heavy, you could use a container to disguise drain covers or unsightly areas to which you need access. Wooden containers tend to weather with age and eventually rot unless you protect them. The most effective and safest way is to paint them with an acrylic-based product, available in a wide range of colors and harmless to plants. With hardwood containers, just brush them with a little teak oil from time to time to keep them fresh.

This plant support consists of thin strips of wood pulled across and interlocked under tension.

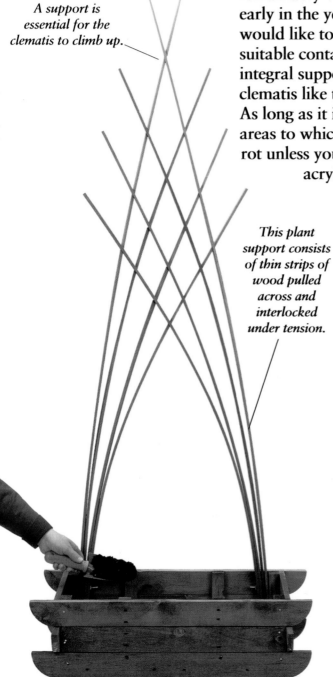

Depending on the size of container, you can plant more than one clematis in it or fill the base with other plants. Montanas and the vigorous species do not do so well in containers as they soon outgrow their pot. The best choices are the large-flowered mid-season varieties with their stunning blooms, the smaller species, such as *C. alpina* and *C. florida*, and some of the more tender, early flowering types, such as *C. forsteri* and *C. armandii*. These last two will do well in a greenhouse, where you can appreciate their scent, even on the coldest days.

2 *Gently lower the clematis into place, with a few buds below the surface, and firm well in. Make sure there are no air gaps around the roots.*

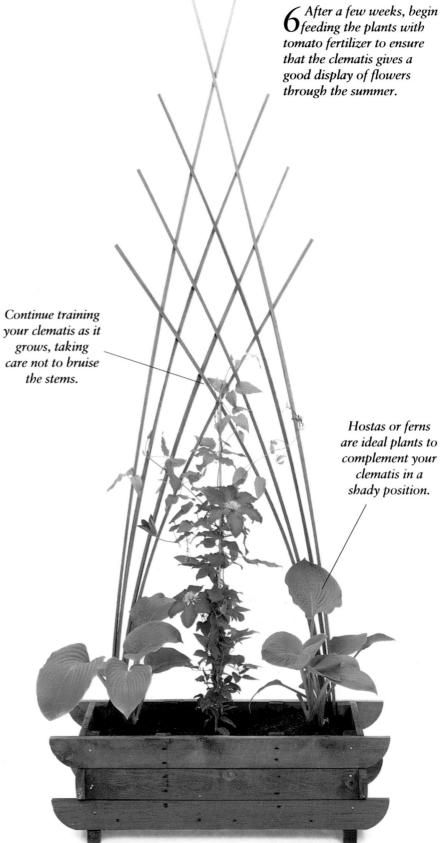

6 After a few weeks, begin feeding the plants with tomato fertilizer to ensure that the clematis gives a good display of flowers through the summer.

4 Gently arrange the clematis shoots around the supports so that they eventually cover as much of them as possible. Loosely secure the shoots, using paper-covered wire plant ties.

5 Water the trough well in at this stage and continue to do so throughout the summer. Wooden, stone and terracotta pots may require more watering than plastic ones.

Continue training your clematis as it grows, taking care not to bruise the stems.

Hostas are particularly attractive to slugs, so place a few slug pellets around the base of each plant to prevent their very large leaves from being damaged.

Hostas or ferns are ideal plants to complement your clematis in a shady position.

3 In this trough, we have used hostas to fill the space around the base of the plant. They make a fine contrast with the clematis and grow exceptionally well in shade, but do require plenty of water to succeed.

Clematis in a large patio container

1 *Choose a potting mixture that will sustain your plants for several years. Clematis grow best in moist, well-drained, fertile soil, and need a cool root run.*

3 *Gently place the clematis into the container close to the supports. Make sure the rootball is not damaged and that some buds will be below soil level.*

2 *Fill the container to within 1in(2.5cm) of the top to allow you to give the plants all the water and feed they require. You can always add more mixture later on if necessary.*

4 *The simplest and least noticeable way of tying your clematis to the support is with paper-covered wire ties. Do not twist these too tight, as you can easily bruise the soft stems.*

This sort of container and its supports were designed primarily for growing runner beans, but it is an admirable means of displaying clematis on the patio. Because of its width, this container holds adequate potting mixture not only for the clematis, but also for a few bedding plants at the base. Here we have used *Begonia semperflorens,* but you could plant any low-growing annual. Alternatively, some of the Mediterranean plants with silver leaves will also thrive at the base of a clematis. Why not try some of the artemisias, such as *Artemisia frigida,* perhaps with some spring crocus underplanted to start the display? When selecting the clematis, avoid the vigorous growing varieties and use the more compact types, such as 'Lady Northcliffe' and 'Comtesse de Bouchaud', as here. The flowering periods of these two varieties flower overlap, which extends the period of interest of the container, and they require different pruning strategies. 'Lady Northcliffe' needs a light prune and 'Comtesse de Bouchaud', a hard prune, but the nature of the supports allows you to do this with ease. Choose your plants carefully; success will depend on the relation of the plants to their location. Remember that the container is open to the weather on all sides and that clematis with very large flowers may well be damaged by any strong summer winds. Finally, bear in mind that a large container complete with potting mixture is heavy, so put the container in its final position before planting.

There are various methods of training clematis. If the plant is growing in a tub against a wall or fence, you could choose a plastic or wooden system available from garden centers. Alternatively, you could make a dome of chicken wire over the container for the clematis to grow through, creating the impression of a potful of flowers. If you choose this method, start with a small plant or cut back a larger plant fairly hard. Another way is to train the clematis plants to spiral around five or six canes. The result is a stunning column of flowers.

7 Continue to water well while the plants establish themselves. They should not dry out. After two to three weeks, feed them with a tomato fertilizer.

8 After about two months, all your efforts will be rewarded with a magnificent show of flowers that will continue to give pleasure throughout the summer.

The flowers should stretch from top to bottom of the supports. These are 'Comtesse de Bouchaud'.

5 Once the clematis are secured, fill the remaining space with plants of your choice, ensuring that both they and the clematis are firmed in well.

Clematis 'Lady Northcliffe' is a compact variety that blooms all summer.

Plants at the base give the container a well-furnished appearance and help to prevent water loss through evaporation.

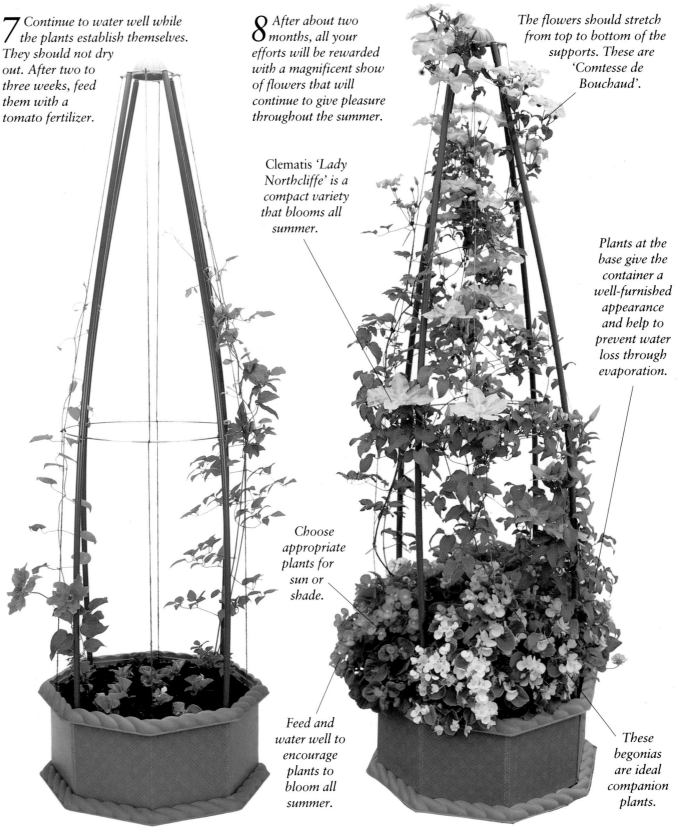

Choose appropriate plants for sun or shade.

6 Water the plants in until some water escapes from the base of the container. If the potting mix is well balanced, overwatering is not a problem.

Feed and water well to encourage plants to bloom all summer.

These begonias are ideal companion plants.

Rich and romantic pinks and reds

The rich burgundies, crimsons and pinks of clematis flowers combine wonderfully well with many summer flowers, including lilies, roses, dianthus and honeysuckle. They provide strong, simple shapes and splashes of solid color, and add texture and richness to any arrangement. For maximum impact, use clematis combined with other blooms in a saturated mix of one color without any contrast or even green foliage. Here, the flowers have been arranged into a rustic wooden bowl with an interesting surface finish that makes them look even richer.

The display includes several different types of clematis, some large-flowered and some small, but they are all in the same color key, from a pale, subtle, grayish pink to deepest velvety maroon. Choose garden flowers to go with the clematis if you have them, such as old-fashioned roses, dianthus and carnations, and add a few exotic pink lilies for their magnificent perfume and stunning shape and color.

4 *Cut pieces of foam to fit inside the bowl and soak them in water. Follow the manufacturer's timing for this. Pack them tightly together in the center of the bowl.*

1 *Cut a circle of plastic to fit, by cutting around the edge of the upturned bowl. An old plastic bag is perfectly suitable for this purpose.*

2 *Turn the bowl the right way up and put the plastic in place. The plastic protects the bowl and retains the water around the arrangement.*

3 *Push the plastic down inside the wooden bowl and smooth it out evenly all round. Obviously it will be somewhat smaller than the bowl, but this is how it is intended to be.*

5 Begin to put areas of flowers into the foam, working from one side to the other. This gives a strong look, rather than dotting the flowers all over.

6 Continue adding flowers to the arrangement, aiming to create a curved, dome-shaped outline above the bowl. This arrangement is designed to be seen from all round.

'Comtesse de Bouchaud' is a pale and pretty pink.

Clematis texensis 'Etoile Rose' has thickly textured, bell-shaped flowers that hang down.

Clematis 'General Sikorski'

Mist the whole arrangement occasionally with a fine spray of water.

7 The finished arrangement would look lovely on a low table or as a centerpiece, particularly against a background of dark, polished wood.

A midsummer mixture

Clematis have a particular way of growing and flowering in the garden. It is best to try to recreate this when making indoor arrangements, rather than forcing the flowers to do something else. This stemmed dish allows the large flowerheads to look quite natural and some can even tumble down to the surface below, as if they were still growing. The rich mix of colors and profusion of blooms makes a spectacular arrangement for any position in the house. Leaving some of the foliage amongst the flowers on the stem provides color contrast and a change of shape and texture, which helps to define the different varieties that have been used. This arrangement is ideal when plenty of flower types are blooming at the same time in midsummer, giving you the opportunity to pick a range of clematis in shades of mauve, purple and burgundy. You could also use a glass cake stand for this idea or even balance a dish or plate on something else to create the same attractive tiered effect.

This clematis is the pale mauve-pink 'Hagley Hybrid'.

1 *Flower foam must be soaked to be really effective. Hold it under the water until it sinks to the bottom. Cut a piece of the wet foam to fit the dish.*

2 *Place the foam in the center of the dish and secure it with special florist's tape designed to work with damp foam. In this case one strip is enough, but add more pieces if you wish.*

3 *Put the first blooms in place, working at the base of the foam and around the display. Consider the angle from which the flowers will be seen.*

There is room to top up the dish with extra water if needed; the lip will stop it overflowing.

Clematis for cutting

Late-flowering, small-flowered clematis seem less likely to wilt once cut, whereas the early-flowering, very large-headed blooms are trickier. Many varieties are particularly suitable for cutting. Some good ones to try are: Pink: 'Dr. Ruppel' and 'Etoile Rose'. Purple: 'The President' and 'Lasurstern'. Mauve: 'Barbara Jackman' and 'Marcel Moser'. Light blue: 'General Sikorski' and 'H.F. Young'. White: 'Moonlight'.

The tumbling foliage adds to the natural effect.

To achieve a lighter finished effect, do not entirely obscure the stem of the dish with blooms.

4 *The finished arrangement looks elegant and stylish. The fact that it is so simple is not obvious at all, but it does rely on perfect blooms at the peak of condition. Stand it out of full sun and enjoy it for several days.*

97

Clematis with sweet honeysuckle

Many of the small-flowered clematis varieties are very suitable for cut flower arrangements and seem to last well in water. Most types bloom from late summer onwards and their lightness and delicacy makes for elegant and stylish designs. In many cases they are easier to use than the very large-headed blooms, which are mostly seen in early summer. Combining them with other flowers or foliage gives you the chance to introduce contrasting colors, flower shapes and textures. Very few clematis varieties have scent except some of the small-flowered species types, so this arrangement mixes the pretty purple *Clematis* x *eriostemon* with a highly scented, pale lemon honeysuckle called 'Graham Thomas'. It is a suitable combination that might just as easily be found in the summer garden, scrambling over a low wall or pergola. The small-flowered types of clematis grow with a mass of flowerheads all together, so it is easiest to pick them in a large trailing piece, with many flowers and buds attached. If the plant is thriving, there will be plenty of stems that can be spared for the house. You can, of course, pick individual blooms, too, for much smaller scale arrangements if you do not want to take much material from the plant.

Once cut, the trails of clematis are prettiest arranged very naturally as if they are still growing. A tall, funnel-shaped, clear glass vase makes a light and delicate container for the clematis. The shape of the vase makes arranging very simple, as the flowers can fan out naturally and form a good rounded shape at the top. Split the thick ends of the cut stems a little way up their length to allow water to be taken up easily. If you do not have a honeysuckle to use with the clematis, you could use any pale or golden yellow flower or shrub, such as solidago, coreopsis, achillea or even yellow roses.

1 *First sort out the flowers and separate out the two types, the clematis and the honeysuckle. Recut their stems at a slanting angle. Fill the vase with water.*

Use freshly drawn, cool water to give the flowers a good start. Make sure that the vase is clean.

2 *Trim away any lower leaves on the stems of honeysuckle, using your fingers or secateurs if you find it easier. Leave a few small leaves at the base of the clematis stems.*

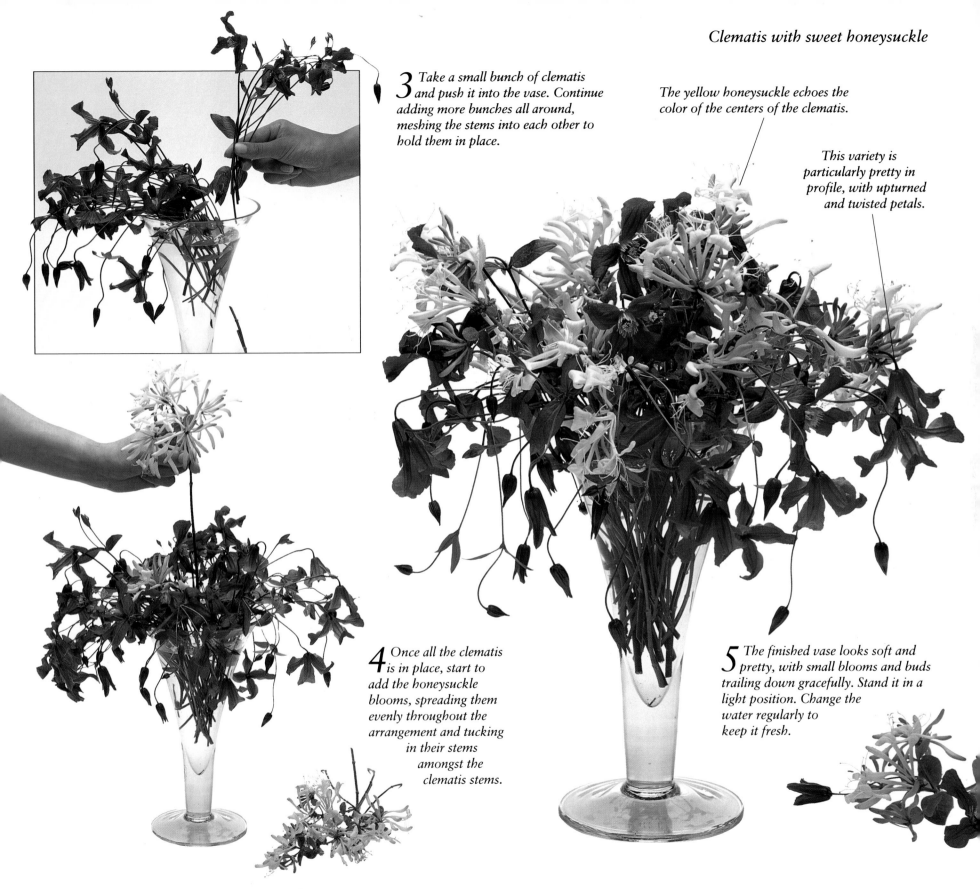

3 Take a small bunch of clematis and push it into the vase. Continue adding more bunches all around, meshing the stems into each other to hold them in place.

The yellow honeysuckle echoes the color of the centers of the clematis.

This variety is particularly pretty in profile, with upturned and twisted petals.

4 Once all the clematis is in place, start to add the honeysuckle blooms, spreading them evenly throughout the arrangement and tucking in their stems amongst the clematis stems.

5 The finished vase looks soft and pretty, with small blooms and buds trailing down gracefully. Stand it in a light position. Change the water regularly to keep it fresh.

99

A late summer classic arrangement

Clematis can be used in the most classical kinds of flower arrangements with great success. Their trailing stems and foliage add interest to more solid flower shapes. There are only a few yellow clematis species, but they are amongst some of the most decorative types and include the pretty *Clematis tangutica* and the subtle, tiny-flowered *Clematis rehderiana*, both used in this arrangement. *C. tangutica* has thick, lemon peel-like petals and small ferny foliage, while *C. rehderiana* has miniature bell-shaped, pale yellowy cream flowers in clusters and smells sweetly of cowslips. Both bloom through late summer onwards. Pick whole pieces of the climbing stem to use for cut flowers or use just single stems of flowers for miniature arrangements. Here the yellows have been mixed with brilliant scarlet crocosmia, nasturtiums and yellow lilies for a spectacular explosion of late summer color.

4 *Now begin to add the larger flowers, such as the yellow lilies, and fill in with nasturtiums and their leaves. A few stems of fennel flowers are also included.*

1 *This classic black vase needs some wire netting to hold the flower stems in place. Cut a piece slightly larger than the neck of the vase and crumple it slightly.*

2 *Put a block of damp flower foam into the vase so that it protrudes slightly. Push the netting over the foam; tuck the edges under the neck of the vase.*

3 *Start by putting a few large pieces of foliage and the stems of crocosmia in place to establish the overall size and shape of the finished arrangement.*

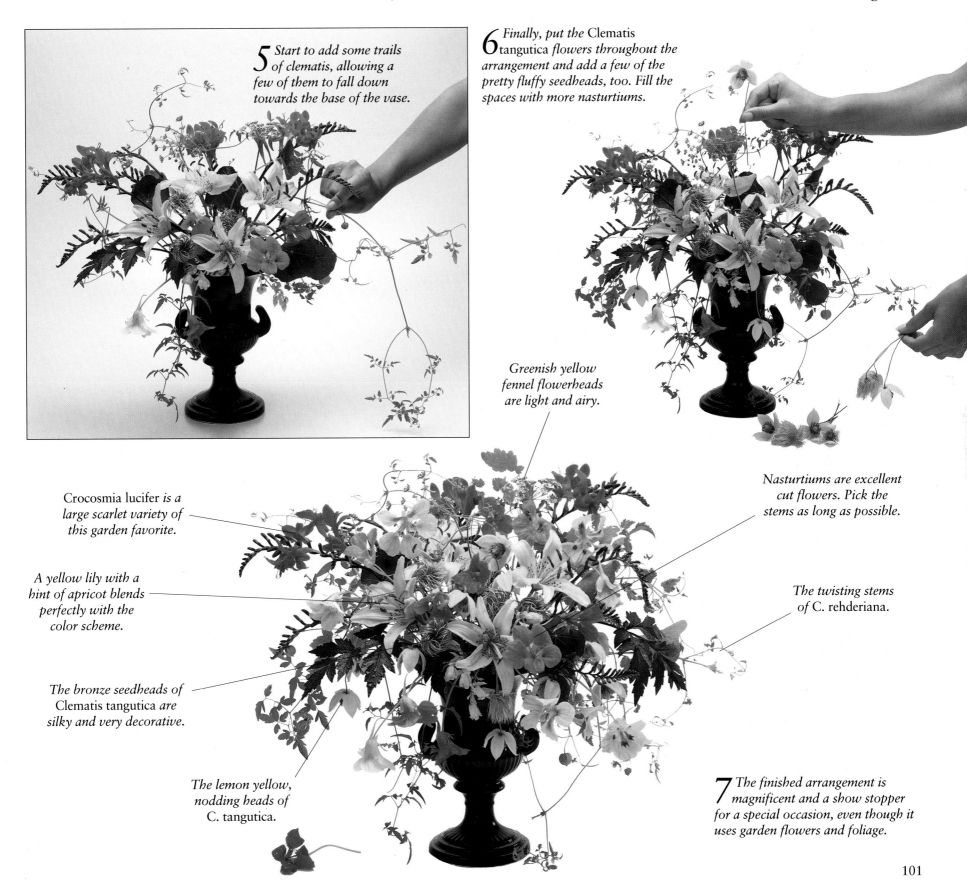

5 *Start to add some trails of clematis, allowing a few of them to fall down towards the base of the vase.*

6 *Finally, put the* Clematis tangutica *flowers throughout the arrangement and add a few of the pretty fluffy seedheads, too. Fill the spaces with more nasturtiums.*

Greenish yellow fennel flowerheads are light and airy.

Crocosmia lucifer is a large scarlet variety of this garden favorite.

Nasturtiums are excellent cut flowers. Pick the stems as long as possible.

A yellow lily with a hint of apricot blends perfectly with the color scheme.

The twisting stems of C. rehderiana.

The bronze seedheads of Clematis tangutica *are silky and very decorative.*

The lemon yellow, nodding heads of C. tangutica.

7 *The finished arrangement is magnificent and a show stopper for a special occasion, even though it uses garden flowers and foliage.*

A country basket of purple and green

Different varieties of clematis mix well together in flower arrangements, and choosing shades of one single color creates a harmonious and pleasing effect. In this display, the acid green of *Alchemilla mollis* has been added to form a contrast that throws the deep purples and mauves of the clematis into relief. The alchemilla flowers also make a good filling material between the clematis flowers, so that they do not have to be crammed too tightly together to fill the space.

Baskets are excellent containers for simple country arrangements and the texture of plaited twigs is always effective in complementing the flowers. Of course, if the basket is not already lined like this one, you will have to line it to make it waterproof, as this arrangement relies on a block of flower foam to hold the stems secure. The display is designed to be seen from all round and slightly from above, so the finished basket would look good on any low table, on a windowsill or as a centerpiece.

4 Once the foam is totally covered, tuck the sweet pea blooms in amongst the alchemilla, spacing them out and working evenly all round the basket.

1 Cut sufficient blocks of flower foam to fill the base of the basket. Make sure that they are thoroughly soaked in water before using them. Follow the maker's instructions.

2 Arrange the foam in a basket lined with plastic or aluminum foil to contain any moisture. Some baskets come ready lined.

3 Start by putting stems of alchemilla across the entire area of foam to make a contrasting background for the clematis.

5 Next, put some of the clematis blooms into the foam, along with a few sprigs of hardy geranium. Mix the light and dark shades of clematis equally throughout the basket.

6 Finally, add some sprigs of fresh, deep purple lavender to fill in any large areas of alchemilla that are not interrupted by other flowers.

A deep burgundy sweet pea mixes well with the other flowers.

7 The finished basket looks natural and relaxed, with a few stems spilling out beyond the edges. It includes an interesting and varied mixture of flowers and foliage.

Rich mauve 'General Sikorski' clematis.

Lime green *Alchemilla mollis* is used as a filler.

A double purple variety of hardy geranium.

Fresh, scented lavender adds a different dimension.

Pink clematis. 'Charisma'

Mixed clematis in a verdigris vase

This small-scale and quite dainty arrangement would be very suitable for a small table, a mantlepiece or any piece of furniture. It is fairly formal in style, because of the elegant, verdigris-finished pottery vase. The narrowness of this vase determines how much material you can put in it, but as the stems of clematis are so thin, it is still possible to fit many different flowers inside without making the display look top-heavy or becoming unstable. To enable you to control where the flowers are positioned, fit a narrow piece of foam into the neck of the vase so that it protrudes a little way above the top edge. Keep an eye on the water level in a vase as small as this, and top it up daily, as the flowers will quickly draw moisture out of the foam. Most of the clematis used here are small-flowered, but there are a few larger ones for interest. A few stems of fresh lavender provide the finishing touch; their spikes contrast well with the softer and flatter clematis blooms.

4 *When you have finished putting all the flowers of the first type of clematis in place, you can begin to add a different variety. Here, pink flowers are mixed in between the purple ones.*

1 *Use a sharp knife to cut a small piece of flower foam to fit the neck of the vase. Soak the foam in water until it is thoroughly wet. Always follow the maker's instructions on preparing the foam for use.*

2 *Push the piece of foam firmly into place, leaving a small amount above the edge of the vase. This adds a little more height to the finished arrangement.*

3 *Start to put one type of clematis into place, spacing the stems out evenly all over the foam. Their height will set the limit to the outline of the arrangement.*

5 When the small clematis are used up, begin to put a few larger flowers in amongst them. For the best effect, do not use more than six to eight larger blooms.

6 Lastly, put in some spikes of fresh lavender, arranging them throughout the display, so that they fill any spaces between the various clematis flowers.

Deep burgundy Clematis 'Niobe' *is rich and velvety.*

Clematis *x* durandii, *a good, deep purple clematis for cutting.*

Fresh lavender adds more variety to the arrangement.

Long-lasting Clematis 'Etoile Rose' *is an excellent cut flower.*

Deep mauve Clematis 'Prinz Hendrick' *has strong stems that are suitable for cutting.*

7 The finished display is neat and compact and densely packed with color and texture. The lavender adds a little scent, as well as welcome contrasting shapes, to the arrangement.

Index to Plants

Credits

The majority of the photographs featured in this book have been taken by Neil Sutherland and are © Colour Library Books. The publishers wish to thank the following photographers for providing additional photographs, credited here by page number and position on the page, i.e. (BL)Bottom left, (TR)Top right, (C)Center, etc.

Pat Brindley: 79(B)

Eric Crichton: 18(B), 19(TL), 21(TL), 30-1(T), 33(B), 34(BL), 44(B), 48(TL), 64(BL), 66(L), 67(R), 68(TR), 76(TL), 77(TR), 79(T), 80, 85(B)

Ron & Christine Foord: 14(TC)

John Glover: Contents page, 15(TR), 16, 17(L), 23(TR), 24(T), 25(TR), 26(BL), 26-7(B), 27(B), 28-9(B), 29(BR), 30(B), 32(TL,TR), 34(R), 35(R), 62, 67(BC), 75(R), 77(TL), 81(BL), 81(T), 82(TR), 82-3(B), 83(R)

Jerry Harpur: 78(BL)

Andrew Lawson: 77(B), 78-9(C)

Clive Nichols Garden Photography: 10, 15(BL), 17(TR,BR), 18(L), 19(R), 20-1(C), 21(R), 22(L), 23(B), 25(B), 27(TL,TR), 28(L,T), 29(T), 31(R), 32(L), 35(TL), 39(TR), 64(R), 68(BC), 68-9(BC), 70(T), 74(TR), 81(BR)

Photos Horticulatural (M & L Warren): 15(BR), 65(L), 66-7(BC), 69(TR), 71(B), 84-5(C), 86(T,B)

Elizabeth Whiting Associates: 87(L)

Wildlife Matters (John Feltwell): 76(BR), 87(R)

Don Wildridge: Half title, 14(BC), 47(TR), 65(R), 82(BL)

Acknowledgments

The publishers would like to thank everyone at Treasures of Tenbury Ltd. who helped during the production of this book, particularly Patricia Cox for preparing the original typescript and Clive Bowes for demonstrating the practical techniques.

GARDEN LIBRARY
PLANTING FIELDS ARBORETUM

SB
413
.C6
H69 H14
1994

Howells, John
HALL, NICHOLAS
Growing clematis

DATE DUE

7/5/17			

GARDEN LIBRARY
PLANTING FIELDS ARBORETUM